EAT YOUR WORDS

EAT YOUR WORDS

A NOVEL

TAYLOR RILEY PARHAM

Copyright © 2024 by Taylor Riley Parham
All Rights Reserved.
ISBN: 979-8-3365-8579-7
Cover by Ever After Cover Design

All brand names and trademarks mentioned in this book are the property of their respective owners. The use of these names is for reference purposes only and does not imply any affiliation with or endorsement by the trademark holders.

This is a work of fiction. Names, characters, places, and incidents either are products of the author's imagination or are used fictitiously. Any resemblance to actual events, locales, or persons, living or dead, is entirely coincidental.

Content Warning:

This novel contains explicit sexual content and strong language. Themes of workplace dynamics and struggles with professional relationships are central to the story, reflecting complex and sometimes challenging interactions. Please read with care.

For my forever best friends,

To Sophia, the one who helped me find my love for Romance, and Kenna, who never failed to make me laugh.
The two of you were my favorite Rom-Com.

Fly high, my beautiful angels.

Acknowledgements

To everyone who has been part of my culinary journey—whether through slider pop-ups or a frozen vending machine—this book is not a recreation of that life but an homage to the industry that has profoundly inspired me.

I am deeply grateful for the experiences and opportunities that have shaped me, and I cherish the moments of creativity and growth I've had in the food world. As I embark on this new journey, I am excited to see where it takes me.

A special thank you to Ever After Cover Design for their incredible artwork. Most importantly, I want to express my heartfelt gratitude to not only my editor–but my inspiration, and my wife.

Forever and always. Bubs & Sug

EAT YOUR WORDS

CHAPTER 1

Riley

"I mean, when you think about it, grapes can be kind of morbid. You get to pick and choose the best ones to eat, over multiple days. Just slowly tearing their family tree apart." After plucking the last grape from the vine and tossing it into a stainless steel bowl full of the rest, I look up to see two pairs of concerned and confused eyes that make me instantly regret opening my mouth.

"What the fuck, Riles?" Joshua's brows raise up at me with a humorous smile as if he can't believe what I just said.

"Okay, well, that's fucking insane. Please don't ever repeat that to a single guest. Let's just call it a refreshing fruit salad that cleanses the palate?" Izzie's hopeful eyes pull me back to reality, and I chuckle. "That sounds great Iz, sorry, you know I'm just bored." I tilt my head and pout my lip, even though I know I'm acting like a baby.

To be fair, I definitely didn't think I'd be making fruit salads after being out of culinary school for 2 years. I should be cooking, baking, roasting, fuck–even plating. Just *anything* other than fruit salads with morbid grapes.

"Oh, we know, you don't refrain from telling us every chance you get." Iz rolls her eyes as she grabs a crate full of fresh veggies and turns around with a fake upset face.

"Oh my God, I can't wait for this to be over with..."
"I'm soooo bored."
"I swear, I'm gonna quit!"

Her mocking is way too accurate. It feels like I'm listening to a recording of myself, but I could never tell her that.

"I don't sound like that. I don't complain *that* much." It sounds like I'm trying to convince myself. I can't be that bad, can I?

"Yes. You do, to both of those," Joshua replies while grabbing and stacking up the rest of the crates before they both leave me to work on this dreadful salad.

Every morning at Wendigo, from 8 a.m. to 11 a.m. we serve our breakfast and brunch menu, which *must* include a dazzling fruit salad. Our salad is more of a fruit display. It contains some of the freshest tropical fruit you can come by, or at least as tropical as it gets in Las Vegas. From dragon fruit and star fruit to pineapples and kiwis, we have it all. It's a beautiful salad, a real showstopper. When I first learned how to make it I thought, "Wow, how can something so basic bring a smile to so many?"

But when you witness it from a guest's point of view, it's like seeing a painting at an art show for the first time. Truly a masterpiece. One that I'm sure I would appreciate more If I wasn't the creator. I've seen this 'masterpiece' every day for an entire year now and I'm over it.

All I see is fruit.

Soon to be brown, rotten, fruit. I've always said the fruit display was beautiful to look at, but it's almost too beautiful. It never gets eaten. No one wants to be the person who destroys the art. It seems like a waste, although everyone in the kitchen would tell me otherwise, but I know they're just being sweet.

I've been stuck making this fruit salad/sculpture every morning for a year now, and it takes 7 hours to prepare. So, yes, it is a waste—a waste of time, passion, and energy. When I was first given the task I took it as an opportunity to show what I was worth. To show that I have the drive, creativity, and love for cooking to do much much more. But I've been trying to build my credibility with Chef Spears for 2 whole years and it has clearly gone nowhere but downhill.

Even with my experience, I started as a prep cook, but I understood that this wasn't school anymore. I was working at a well-known restaurant that serves almost 2,000 people a week. They had to trust me, so I took my time—not that I had the choice.

I became close with the front-of-house staff. Iz, our best waitress and my best friend/roommate. Joshua is our best server who is extremely loud, gay, and proud. The team of two run Wendigo, without them even Spears knows the restaurant wouldn't last. Without them, I wouldn't even have this opportunity. They both helped to get me to the position I am in today, even if that is just a fruit salad maker.

...

After a long day of watching my fruit display die and preparing for my next one that will be served tomorrow, I head out to meet up with Josh and Iz at our favorite spot, Charlie's.

While Wendigo may be known for its prestigious brunch that celebrities can't get enough of, nothing will ever beat Charlie's, and everyone knows it. It's a local classic that has been around for over 40 years, it's irreplaceable. Josh and Iz are probably there, already 3 tacos and 2 margaritas deep.

My assumptions are proven right when I walk in. The first thing I see is both of them chugging what looks to be mango margaritas before slamming them down on the bar, almost breaking their glasses.

"Woah there! Is this a race or something?" I interject their conversation by pulling a stool out and sitting on the other side of Iz.

"Heyyyy!!!" Joshua's eyes widen in surprise and Iz whips around toward me.

"You made it!" Both of their smiles make me happy that I got extra work done so I can spend more time with them.

"Of course. I'm starving, and I need this if I'm going to make it through another week with Spears," I mutter while Joshua is already waving down the waiter, probably ordering us 3 more drinks.

"You say that every week Riles. You need to relax and trust the process." Iz is *over* hearing about it–everyone is.

"Yeah, well, the process isn't really *processing* right now. I want to create 5-star dishes Iz, not fruit art." The sigh I let out could be heard for miles.

"I get that Riles, but do you think Spears just woke up and was handed everything? No, he had to get up and take it." Izzie's tone is firm, which is surprising since she's been drinking, but I guess my choice of topics can be sobering.

"You don't think I get up every day and take it?" My brows furrow in confusion because my body would beg to differ. Every time I bend in any direction my bones sound like a box of dry pasta being crushed.

"I didn't say get up and *work*. Of course, you do–but do you get up, grab life by its reins, and take what you want?"

I sit there in silence with all eyes on me. I've never thought about it. How am I supposed to take what I want? If you had asked me a year ago how I felt about where I was in life, I would've said I was content. Just a year prior, I had graduated from school and was immediately hired as a prep cook at one of the most sought-after restaurants today. I felt accomplished like I reached a lifelong dream, but now that dream seems so minuscule. I went from a prep cook to arranging fruit displays. Something about that feels backward.

For years, I blamed Spears. Granted, he's my boss and hasn't let me make a single dish, but I also never spoke up. I'm afraid of losing everything I've worked so hard to build, and it's led to burnout. I know I've lost some of my passion along the way. Maybe Iz is right—maybe I'm letting this happen *to* me. Maybe it's time for me to let myself win.

Before I can respond, their third round and my first arrive at the table, and I couldn't be happier.

I grab the stem of the glass and raise it up high, without questioning, Joshua and Iz both do the same.

"Here's to me taking what the fuck I want!" I accentuate every syllable with a huge grin on my face because I can't contain how I feel right now. The inspiration is already flowing, the energy's rising, and the thrill is slowly creeping back to me.

My energy is matched when two glasses crash into mine.

"To taking what the fuck we want!!" They scream it much louder than I do. But I don't even care, because I'm back.

CHAPTER 2

Riley

"R iley!"

The smell of the garlic roasting has to be my favorite scent, there's nothing like it. In culinary school, they taught us that no matter what we're cooking, throw some garlic in a pan and your customers will line up at the door.

"Rileyyy!"

But this garlic smells too good to be real like it's been roasting for hours.

"Riley, wake uuup!"

Wait, it isn't real.

"DUDE!"

The harsh reality hits me like a wave when I feel the crash of a fluffy cloud slapping me across the face. I spring up so fast It immediately makes me dizzy.

"Fuck, Izzie." I hold my throbbing head, it's so bright in my room that I can barely open my eyes to squint at a panicked Iz.

"You have to get to work, I know you prepped extra last night, but not enough to miss a day!"

I hear every word she's saying but my thoughts are still loading. I guess I'm taking too long to gather myself because Izzie is already ripping my comforter off my body.

"It's already 6:30, brunch is at 8:00 Riles, come onnnn!" She shakes my bed one final time, not helping my headache.

And then everything hits me like a ton of bricks—Wendigo.

"Ohhhh, fuck me!" I jump out of bed faster than I can think and I'm racing to the bathroom to fix my appearance.

"No thanks, but hurry up, I'll meet you by the car in ten." I barely chuckle at Iz because I'm too busy detangling my hair.

I definitely slept in this morning. After my first round of margaritas, I *think* I had 5 more, but I don't remember much after that.

Okay, well, I might not be fully *back* just yet but I'm getting there.

...

Honestly, if it was any other day, my being late wouldn't be the worst thing that has happened. But as I walk into Wendigo, and Iz heads in a different direction to help the staff in front; I turn and round the corner to the kitchen only to come crashing right into the man himself, Chef Spears.

"Oh, what the fuck!?" All of the fresh produce that was in the crates Spears was carrying flew across the room, and I could feel my face turn as bright red as the now dirty tomatoes in front of me.

"What the fuck, Bennett?!" I don't even need to meet his eyes to know they're shooting daggers into my skull.

After a moment of shock, I immediately drop to my knees and scramble around grabbing anything that I can.

"Oh my god, I'm so so sorry, I didn't see yo–"

"Of course you didn't, because you aren't where you're supposed to be! Shouldn't you be prepping fruit, Bennett?" Fuck, he knows I'm late. I rush to my feet as I stammer over my words.

"I...uh..." I can't even get anything to come out of my mouth, I feel so pathetic. My shoulders slump in desperation and just then I feel a hand reach around me and I look up to see Joshua already grabbing the crate from my hands.

"She stayed late last night prepping for today's display so she wouldn't have to be here as early as the rest of us, Chef," Joshua says confidently while walking away—swiftly as if he didn't just do what I couldn't manage in a million years: stand up to Spears. But for Joshua and Iz, this is second nature. They've been in the customer service industry for way longer and can handle egotistical dicks like Spears. For me, though, this isn't going to be some overnight change.

Because the Spears I'm standing in front of right now, definitely doesn't value me, or see me as anything more than what I do today.

"Hmm, well, don't let this become a recurrence. I don't need *my* team thinking they can show up at any time, understood?" Emphasizing the fact that I'm not included in that 'team'. He raises a brow to see if I'll take the bait and argue.

"Understood." I don't bite. I don't make any eye contact as he shoves past me.

"Clean this up, the team meeting is in an hour!" he barks.

I drop back down and fight back tears as I shove all of the useless produce back into its crate. Within seconds, another pair of knees are on the ground next to me and I raise my watery eyes to see Kenzie, a young waitress who just started working at Wendigo two months ago, but already accustomed to Spears' demeanor.

"Hey, don't worry about it, I think Spears is just mad because his food delivery is coming later than expected." Kenzie bumps my shoulder and starts to help me clean up. I chuckle lightly at her comment because she's probably not wrong. It wouldn't be the first time Spears took his anger out on someone passing through.

"Yeah, well, I'm sure me coming in later than usual didn't help." We both stand up, each holding a crate, and head to the back towards the dumpsters.

"I wouldn't think too much about it though, I heard we have good news for this team meeting so hopefully it will help lighten his mood!" Kenzie tosses both crates in the dumpster while I hold the back door open, and we both head back in with the hope that the day will get better.

...

After another morning of precisely placing fruit in its assigned spot with toothpicks and hot sugar as glue, today's sculpture is a beautiful edible floral arrangement. Roses are made from fresh strawberries that have been dipped in hot sugar to preserve their structure and Peonies that have been hand-carved from honeydew, which can only be done the day of because of how quickly their colors change. The two combined create a breathtaking arrangement that would brighten anyone's morning. I catch myself smiling because I know I put some actual energy into this display.

"Damn, Bennett, I see youuu!" Did Spears scare some energy into you?!" I turn and see a smiling Alex walking toward me.

I laugh and turn back to my display "Something like that."

"Shit, I need some of whatever it is you're on, this damn butternut squash isn't getting soft enough for me to purée. I told Spears I roasted them last night thinking I could get them done quickly this morning, but now everything's off schedule."

He sighs, still looking ahead and we both just burst into laughter.

"Fuck, Spears is going to be pissed," I say in between breaths of laughter, we're both practically bent over holding our stomachs at this point.

"He's already pissed, fuck it!" But the way Alex still whispers his words as if he doesn't want Spears to hear him, sends us into another fit of laughter. And it was at that moment I realized I hadn't laughed this hard at work in a long time.

"Okay, Mr. and Mrs. Chuckles, it's time for the team meeting, you coming?" Iz comes around the corner raising her eyebrows at us, questioning our weird actions, but is soon distracted by my display.

"Holy shit, Riles, you just did this?" Her gumball-sized eyes and dropped jaw make me laugh again.

"Yeah," I say as we both just smile at each other and Izzie's proud look makes me feel like my actions are finally matching my words.

"Okay, gay birds, let's get to the meeting before we don't have jobs, yeah?" Alex grabs both of our arms and pushes us to start walking toward the back office, and we all laugh at the actual high probability of one of us being fired for being late.

Our meeting begins with Joey, our office manager, and Chef Spears' assistant (bless her poor heart) going over our expectations for this weekend's rush.

We have two weekly meetings, one on Mondays to plan our week and another on Thursdays to plan our weekends.

We have 3 high-profile guests coming on Saturday for Brunch. They plan on filming an episode of *Keeping Up with the Kennedys*, and we always make special accommodations to help the flow of the restaurant run smoothly while filming.

We also have a reservation from Mike Dyson and his team for this Sunday evening. Which usually means staying open later than normal to give our "top-tier guests" as Chef Spears would say, the best experience possible.

If we don't prioritize their comfort over everything else–our business is over. I mean it's Vegas, we all rely on high-profile celebrities or businessmen to come to Vegas and spend big bucks. Then go home and leave us a glamorous review that entices all of their fans to come to our restaurant.

As Joey goes over the schedule, Chef Spears, as usual, cuts her off to go on a rant about how we need to be quicker getting the appetizers out. Apparently, he believes we should prep and freeze the appetizers to get them out faster and our customers will be too drunk off of our overpriced wine to know the difference. It just makes me think about what Izzie said to me last night. If this dumbass can open a restaurant in Vegas, why can't I get what I want?

"And another thing, who signed for that case of herbs last week?" He doesn't even let anyone speak up before continuing.

"They were limper than my Grandpa's dick! Like seriously, you guys come on!" He whips his head around looking at all of us with those same crazy wide eyes he gets whenever his blood pressure starts to rise.

"Wellll...bringing it back to this weekend. Have you made up your mind on that *Foodie* article? You'd have to be there this Saturday." Joey swiftly changes the subject but Spears looks more upset than before.

"Oh, Fuuuuuck no! I don't have time for that shit, we have 2 high profile groups coming this weekend!" He jumps up from his chair and starts pacing, if we all didn't want to leave before we sure as hell do now.

"What the hell am I supposed to do?" He looks at Joey as if she has all the answers.

"I don't know, I've been bugging you for weeks on this, but you can't back out. They're naming you "Hottest New Chef Today."

Before Spears can look at her, with hopeful eyes she finishes "And no, I can't go in your place, I have to be here with the producer for Saturday's filming of KUWTK."

Joey raises her brows and gives him an 'I told you so' look, and Spears rolls his eyes in return while nibbling on his bottom lip, deep in thought.

As much as I'd love to save this moment to laugh at later at night, my mind is somewhere else and I can't stop myself when my mouth opens and says;

"I can go!"

CHAPTER 3

Riley

"What do you *mean*, you can go?"

I don't know what came over me, and I've never regretted saying something faster, because the amount of surprised and confused eyes looking back at me has me choking up again as I try to to respond to Spears, but I clear my throat and somehow continue.

"Uhhhh...well, if you know *you* can't go, and Joey can't either. So, I just thought I would offer...my help?" It comes out more like a question, but I look across the room to see Joshua's amused but impressed expression that makes me slightly relax.

A scoff across the room draws my attention past everyone else's still-shocked faces to an unimpressed Chef Spears.

"As sweet as your little hero moment seems, they want a *real* chef for this article, and I highly doubt they'll be delighted to see a newbie prep cook as my replacement." As usual, his words cut a deep wound but instead of letting my shoulders drop into their usual place of defeat, I raise my chin to meet his eyes and challenge him.

"Well, do you have anybody else?" I ask, watching his eyebrows shoot up at my response. The suppressed chuckles around me don't go unnoticed, but I keep my eyes fixed on Chef Spears.

A loud, but cheerful voice breaks our stare-off and we both turn to face Joey who looks like she just found a golden ticket.

"Oh my god! This works out perfectly, can you leave this Saturday?" And this time it's my eyebrows that shoot up at her eagerness.

"Joey come on?! You can't be serious right now? *Her*?!" Spears looks at Joey like she's losing her mind.

"I'm dead fucking serious Spears. You don't really have another option right now, and every time I even bring up this article, you can't stop yapping on about this damn editor. You can't stand her anyway, so just let someone else do it!"

I snap my head towards Spears who's already glaring at me, but he redirects his attention back to Joey.

"Because she's just some raging, gay feminist who thinks she knows the food industry better than *actual* chefs. She barely even responded to my emails when I invited her out here to check out Wendigo!" Spears shouts in response. But Joey only tightens her lips and tilts her head.

"Maybe it's because you choose to refer to her as a 'raging gay feminist' when her name is Eden Turner. And secondly, she's a damn New York Times Best Selling Author, she doesn't have time for *your* crap." Nobody can hold in their laughter after that, but Spears doesn't even care.

At this point, his head is tossing around out of frustration, and for the first time, he seems overwhelmed with his little-to-no options. Compared to his work, it's interesting to see him act completely out of control and helpless.

"And Riley *is* technically a Chef, she just hasn't been given an opportunity to really grow."

Joey saying this in front of everyone should make me feel embarrassed, but surprisingly more than anything I feel heard.

Spears scoffs again, "Please–I've given her plenty of chances." He can't look me in the eye this time, maybe it's because he knows it's partly bullshit.

And Joey's face confirms my thoughts when she tilts her head and raises one brow.

"Also, not to interrupt, but you do need us here for dinner service this weekend." My head snaps to Alex who's already winking back at me, almost knowing I need this win.

Spears drops his hands from his hair and lets out a loud groan.

"Fucking hell, fine. What-fucking-ever at this point!!" My eyes widen when he turns and faces me head-on.

"I'm giving you this *one* chance, you fuck this up and you're done, Bennett. Understood?"

And without thinking about it another second I respond.

"Understood."

CHAPTER 4

Riley

"Cheers to Riley, for taking what the fuck she wants!"

A roar of cheers, clinking glasses, and excited screams make my huge smile grow even bigger as I raise my glass for my fourth tequila shot of the night.

The Bare Bar is where we go to get fucked up and celebrate any pointless accomplishments. So it's the perfect spot to celebrate my newfound confidence.

About 30 minutes ago, I was sitting in my favorite booth with Joshua and Iz, but at this point, we're dancing with anyone who passes through.

"Riley, you're going to New-fucking-York, what the actual fuuuuck?!?" Joshua has said it ten times since we arrived, but it still hasn't clicked for me. I know I'm probably running off of straight adrenaline, but I'm hoping it turns into something more solid by Saturday. Right now, I don't want to think about the what-ifs, I just want to hold onto this feeling of finally putting myself out there.

I giggle and throw my head back letting out a much-needed sigh from today's wave of emotions. "Shit, I don't even know what just happened today," I say genuinely shocked with myself.

"You put yourself first Riles, that's what happened! And on Saturday you're going to be over 2,000 miles away, sitting pretty with fucking food editors!!" Just for a moment, everything stops. The music is low and muffled, and the only thing I heard Iz say was "*Saturday.*"

Fuck, Saturday. My face must show my shift of emotions because Joshua and Iz are both grabbing my arms to pull me out of my head.

"Oh, no you don't. You didn't just stand up to 'Chef Limp Dick' today for no reason. Don't start overthinking everything; we're here to celebrate!" Joshua reassures me, and Iz squeezes my hand as she nods in agreement.

The tension in my body releases like gas in a can and I return a smile.

They're right, I didn't speak up for no reason, it was supposed to happen. I can work out the details later, tonight I need to relish in this moment.

So without pushing it further, I toss back my fifth shot, and as the tequila burns my throat I close my eyes to imagine the alcohol burning all of my fears of what's to come into ash.

...

That dream only lasts so long, because when I wake up Friday morning everything hits me like a bus.

Oh. My. God. I'm going to fucking New York.

I started my day off by pacing, much like Chef Spears did when he realized he couldn't go. How ironic?

With each step I take, I replay every second of my stupid decision to put myself first. Because now I have to keep up this act of confidence. I know all I'm doing is answering questions about Wendigo and the dishes we've made for years, but I'm covering for a chef, an *actual* chef.

Of course, I graduated from culinary school and technically I *am* a chef too. But I graduated two years ago, and within those years I have nothing to show for it, I have no portfolio. That's why I'm just a chef based on my qualifications, not my work.

And on Saturday morning, I'll have to get up go on a fucking plane to New York, and act like I actually know what the hell I'm doing. I mean come on, I've only made fruit displays for the past year. I have the right to pace, and I also have the time, seeing as Spears reluctantly gave me Friday off to prepare for my flight.

As time passes, my pace quickens, and what feels like minutes stretches into hours of dragging my feet and my fears.

By the time Iz gets home, she finds me standing in front of my empty suitcase with my head in my hands.

"Oh nooo, how long have you been standing there, Riley?" I don't even turn around to reply.

"I don't even know at this point, but I spent all day pacing around like a dumbass, and now I don't even have time to figure any of this out!" At this point, I'm on the verge of tears and I just want to drop to the ground to let everything swallow me up whole. That would probably still be easier than anything else.

But the unforgettable smell of the cleaner we use at Wendigo envelopes me when Izzie's arms wrap around me to stop the tears waiting at the brim of my eyes.

"Oh, Riles, I knew you were going to be here overthinking everything, but you need to think of this as a vacation!" My tears have never stopped quicker, I almost start laughing at the thought.

"A *vacation*? What about me having to interview as Chef Spears for a *Foodie* article sounds like a vacation to you?" I rip away from her grasp and continue.

"Not to mention me having to work with a possibly very rude editor, I mean if Spears thinks she's rude, then what does that say? He did say something about her not being straight, you know how critical gays can be!"

I let out a breath as I finished, not even realizing how fast I was talking. As soon as Iz sees I'm done, she raises her pointer finger and starts speaking.

"First of all, not only do you get to be out of the kitchen for a week, but you're literally flying to New York City to talk about your favorite thing ever– food. Secondly, if she hates Spears so much then you two might actually already have something in common. And third, bitch, you're Bisexual, which makes you just as critical as her. But right now, you're worse–judging without even meeting her!" Izzie's eyebrows shoot up as she crosses her arms.

Fuck, she's right. Again. I am acting judgy, not that that's unusual, but I'm normally only over-critical of myself. And how could I possibly criticize her when she's the editor of *Foodie*?

As if on cue, she says "Yeah, I know I'm right." Izzie's sick smile never fails to piss me off.

"Okay, but this still doesn't solve my clothes problem–" I turn back around to face the empty suitcase and pile of clothes that has gathered on my floor. "–I can't go there in any of *this*, all I have is chef coats in every shade, and basic tees."

Iz steps up next to me and immediately laughs.

"Uhhh...yeah, the old college closet isn't gonna cut it." I burst into a fit of laughter because it's so accurate. The pile of clothes is made up of old graphic tees and ripped jeans that are beyond faded. Damn, I guess I still haven't upgraded any of my clothes since school. I just figured what's the point if the clothes still fit, and I haven't really gotten the chance to go shopping since I work full time.

"Hold on—" Iz runs in and out of both our rooms for the next fifteen minutes, laying out and arranging multiple outfits that I probably won't even get a chance to wear since I'll be in a chef coat half the time. Still, I'm in awe; Iz has always had great style, and I never thought in a million years I'd be wearing her clothes to New York.

"Iz, what the fuck? This is insane, and you know it?" I stare, dumbfounded, as she finishes styling the last outfit, a skin-tight black midi dress. It's one of Izzie's most prized possessions. She bought it a year ago for her birthday and only wears it for "special occasions"–special occasions meaning if she's getting laid.

I turn to Iz, confused. "Okay, now this is all beautiful, but why in the world would I need your 'fuck me' dress?" A mischievous smirk begins to grow on Izzie's face.

"This is for the night you decide to really step out of your comfort zone and give yourself not just what you want—but what you *need*." My confusion grows, but as her eyebrow raises, as if I'm supposed to understand, everything suddenly clicks, and my face turns bright red.

"IZ! OH MY GOD!" I cover my face with my hands as I hear her chuckle.

"Well, I'm just saying Riles, you never know!" I watch in horror as she squeezes her 'fuck me' dress into my suitcase next to a pair of heels.

As much as I'd like to argue the fact that I don't plan on stepping that far out of my comfort zone just yet, all I can think about is how lucky I am to have people in my life who care this much about me.

"Thank you, Iz" is all I can muster before my tears from earlier pile back up, and I'm grabbing Iz for another hug.

"Of course, now let's get some rest, you've got a big day tomorrow."

We both finished packing and for the first time today, I actually sat down. I can feel the weight of the day sitting on my eyelids and as I slowly give in, I let the flow of next week's possibilities float in and out of my dreams.

...

"Okay, here we are. Have a nice trip! And please leave me a rating if you can!"

I roll my eyes and almost scoff at the *Hoover* driver I booked for my ride to the airport. Not only was he speeding, but he was on the phone the entire ride. And he only spoke to me once we pulled up to my terminal.

I hop out of the car, ready to throw up from the intense motion sickness.

"Righhhht." I close the door after I grab my suitcase and he's already down the street before I even get onto the sidewalk. Fuck, some people are just not meant to drive.

But I immediately forget about the ride as soon as I make it inside the airport and remember what I'm actually here for.

This morning, before I left, Joshua came over so we could all have a super early breakfast together. Besides the *Hoover* fiasco, I've been surprisingly calm. Joshua even said it was kind of scary, and all I could do was laugh.

As I scan the airport, I finally spot the check-in desk and head straight to where a sweet older lady with a pixie cut and a bright smile stands.

"Hello, can I help you check in your suitcase for your flight today, Ma'am?" She tilts her head and looks at me with the warmest eyes that could make anyone melt.

"Uhh...yeah, my name is Riley Bennett. I believe my flight is for 6:45 a.m.?" I scramble trying to fish around for my ID.

She begins typing in my name as I slide my ID across the counter, "Oh, yes, here you are dear, but the flight is actually for 5:45, they've been boarding for the past 20 minutes." My heart stops and I can feel my ears starting to ring.

"WHAT?" The sudden realization hits that Chef Spears told me 6:45 for his flight instead.

"Oh, it's going to be okay dear, If you want to leave your suitcase on his scale here you can go ahead and start heading to your gate. I'm just going to call it in on the intercom, and they'll wait for ya. Besides, sugar, you've got fir—" I don't even let her finish. Dropping my suitcase, I sprint toward security.

Before I get too far, I glance back over my shoulder and shout, "Thank you!" The sweet lady is already smiling and waving back at me.

Somehow, after making it through TSA quickly (maybe it was because I had Pre-Check for the first time ever) I made it to my gate just in time. After getting my ticket scanned, I find myself still running down the ramp and onto the plane, only to realize I have no idea where my seat is.

I whip my ticket out from the back pocket of my jeans as I make my way past smiling flight attendants, I smile back and quickly redirect my attention to my ticket, which reads *C6*.

"Hmmm, C6," I say to myself. I begin walking down the aisle saying "Excuse me" every couple of steps, and whipping my head from left to right trying to read the seat numbers. I look down for one second to reread my ticket, and I trip over something that sends me face-first crashing onto the floor of the plane.

CHAPTER 5

Riley

I don't know how long I've been lying on the ground with my eyes closed, silently praying I wake up from this sick nightmare. But when I finally take a peek at my reality, I'm met with the nicest loafers I've ever seen: they're shiny, black, lined with light-brown fur, with a small gold designer logo on top. Shit, these look expensive.

As I take in the black slacks and a matching blazer that look just as expensive as the shoes, I'm jolted back to reality when someone clears their throat. Fuck, I'm still on the ground. I start to push myself up on the palms of my hands when another hand suddenly appears in front of me—this one is tan, smooth, and adorned with gold rings that perfectly match the gold on the loafers.

"Uhh...you okay?" My eyes shoot up to see where the soft, but slightly raspy voice was coming from. I shouldn't be surprised, since the outfit alone should've told me how beautiful she was going to be, but holy shit, I can't help but stare in awe. All of a sudden, I think I understand what my guests at Wendigo feel when they look at my displays and say that they're too beautiful to touch.

Her eyes are the brightest brown I've ever seen, almost hazel—but not quite. The dark brown surrounding them creates a perfect ombré, making them entrancing. And her bone structure is so strong it's surreal, but her lips and curls seem to soften everything.

My thoughts are cut short again when I notice her perfectly bushy eyebrows shoot up as if she knew I was staring.

"You gonna grab my hand, or stay there the whole flight?" she teases. "A smirk starts to appear on her face as I quickly reach up to grab her way-too-soft-to-be-real hand and pull myself up.

"Uhhh...thank you so much. So sorry about that!" I try not to look her in the eyes because I know my face is beet red. I glance down and see not only my untied shoelace, likely the culprit of my disaster but also my ticket.

Just as I reach down to pick it up, the mysterious yet intimidatingly beautiful woman beats me to it. As she quickly scans over my ticket, I'm too stunned to speak, standing there like a lost puppy waiting for instructions.

"Hmm, well looks like you fell at the right spot 'cause you're right next to me." Her smile widens as my eyes do the same but in confusion. My head whips around to take in my surroundings. This is still first class.

"Huh?" I rip the ticket from her hands and read over it again.

C6.

I look up at the empty row of 2 seats in front of me and see C5 and C6.

Holy shit, I'm in fucking first class. How is this possible?

"You gonna sit down at any point? I think the flight attendants are about to come yell at us." I see her hand pointing toward the empty seats, and when I glance over my shoulder, I notice a flight attendant approaching us.

"Oh yeah, sorry." I began to awkwardly scoot past her seat to my window seat, perfect for avoiding eye contact.

When I look back up the flight attendant has disappeared, and I sigh gratefully.

This is all way too much. In a matter of seconds, I went from being late and face down on the ground to sitting in first class with the most beautiful woman I've ever seen.

As she sits down next to me I can confirm she smells just as good as she looks. It's layered, but it only takes my chef nose a few seconds to decipher the main notes; vanilla, coffee, and musk. God, could she get any more perfect?

I make the mistake of turning to my left just to sneak a peek because my eyes are stuck on her side profile. I can hear the flight attendants begin their safety protocol but I'm too mesmerized by her jaw to pay them any mind. But I quickly snap my head back to the window when she starts to notice my gaze. Luckily, she doesn't say anything and I can drown in embarrassment silently.

As the plane leaves the runway, I'm reminded of why I'm on this flight to begin with. And Izzie's words from last night replay in my head.

"You need to think of this as a vacation."

This does kind of already feel like a vacation, and I do have Izzie's entire closet in my suitcase. It will be my first time in New York, where there are way too many restaurants there on my bucket list to try. Something inside me is urging me to let go and relax—it's finally time for me to have some fun.

For the first time in ten minutes, after contemplating my life while staring out the window, I muster the courage to turn and press the call button. I avoid looking beside me to keep from backing out. When the flight attendant arrives, I finally glance up and see that she's completely focused on her laptop, propped up on the table in front of her, and doesn't seem the slightest bit concerned about me. She looks like she's typing something serious as I watch her jaw clench, and I feel a wave of something come over me, but it's interrupted by the flight attendant clearing her throat this time.

Fuck, I was staring again.

"Can I get you anything?" Her brows are raised as she waits for me to get my shit together.

"Umm, do you have any champagne by chance?" I immediately feel another pair of eyes on me but I refuse to meet them.

"Yes, of course." She smiled at me and walked away swiftly. Whew, that went smoothly.

She returns just as quickly as she left with one glass of champagne and she reaches over to pass it to me.

"Our champagne is complimentary in first class, enjoy your flight!" She winks at me and walks away in the opposite direction.

Fuck, free drinks? I can feel my body start to relax as I take my first sip and my throat immediately warms up. Now *this* is what I call a vacation.

...

For the first hour of the flight, I consume 3 glasses of FREE champagne and listen to the sounds of the mystery model next to me typing. I can't help but steal glances at her every chance I get, and I know I'm getting less and less sneaky with it as the drinks start to add up. By the time I'm almost finished with my third drink, I'm practically full-on staring with my body tilted towards her. And yet she still seems to pay me no mind, *Tipsy Me* doesn't like the silence.

I start to fidget around and get angsty, almost like how a child moves when they want attention. I'm never like this, I like to be behind the scenes. I'd rather make fifty fruit displays than have to be in the front and talk to the customers. And I sure as hell don't throw a fit when I don't get attention. So why do I feel like her not giving me any is actually pissing me off? I don't even know her, but when I watch her jaw clench for the 5th time I can't stop myself from opening my mouth to speak.

But instead of just speaking calmly I blurt "Who wears a suit on a plane?" The feeling of regret seeps in as soon as her head snaps to me, her eyebrows shooting up at my random comment.

Her brown eyes scan my face before lightly chuckling, "I just came from a meeting in Vegas, and technically I wouldn't really call this a suit–" she reaches behind herself moving her blazer out of the way so I can see the elastic waistband she's pulling on. But I'm focused on the tattoo I see peeking out from under her shirt. "–I had my tailor custom fit it to be more comfortable to be worn on planes."

I scoff at the fact she has a job that requires a tailor to make her a custom "comfy" suit. And because she could probably wear a trash bag, and it would look like it was made for her.

"Geez, you just left a meeting, to get on a plane and type your life away?"

What in the world has gotten into me? Why the hell am I pushing it?

Luckily she just laughs, sighs, and turns to face me. I really wish she didn't though, because now I can't focus on anything else. Her perfectly pouty lips are slightly redder than what I'm guessing is usual because she's been chewing on them for the past hour. I would know because I turn every time she does it, without fail.

"I'm a writer, this is literally what I do." She shrugs her shoulders and I can't help but giggle because of course she's a mysterious writer.

"Sorry, it's just that I should've expected it, you give off rich, mysterious writer vibes." Now only one brow is raised as I stare comically.

"But you must be writing something good if you haven't stopped for a second to breathe," I quickly add.

That makes her scoff and turn back to her laptop. "Trust me, there's nothing special about this, I just have a deadline to finish this article." I lean forward, closer to her, my interest heightened.

I'm intrigued.

"Oohhh, an article, would I know any of your work?" I smile softly as she looks at me like she's contemplating something.

"Probably not, I only write small stuff." My eyes squint at her because something tells me she definitely doesn't only write "small stuff." But I don't push any further because I know I've done enough damage. I sit back and click my 'press to call' button for the fourth time so far. And when the same flight attendant from earlier comes down she's already carrying another glass of champagne.

"I'm guessing you are ready for another?" She smiles warmly as she passes it to me.

"Yes, and actually can I get another for her?" I don't look down to see the eyes burning into mine because so far, no eye contact has worked for me.

"Oh, of course, I'll be right back!" she walks away before either of us can reply, and my attention is forced back to the hot writer next to me.

"I'm sorry, I just can't be the only one chugging down glasses of champagne." I come up with an excuse, trying to hide the fact that I just really want her to talk to me more.

She laughs as she closes her laptop. My smile grows ridiculously wide as I realize I've captured the attention of the random writer. It broadens further when I see her grab the drink from the flight attendant and take her first sip, noting how she visibly relaxes.

"Honestly, I needed this, thank you." She smiles back at me and re-adjusts in her seat to face me again, fuck.

"So, I've told you what I do; what about you?" she asks lightly. My body freezes, and I'm reminded of my less-than-stellar career as a fruit sculptor. I clear my throat, preparing to explain my seemingly insignificant life in Vegas, already feeling the shift in energy and the onset of embarrassment. But then something in me shifts and the only thing I can think of is when Alex was next to me and said *"Fuck it."*

So I straighten my shoulders and raise my chin, "Oh, I'm a chef."

CHAPTER 6

Riley

"You know, you kind of remind me of James Bond."

My unwavering stare makes her chuckle and set down her (I don't even know what number at this point) drink.

She tosses her endless curls, which I've been staring at for far too long. I already asked her how she gets them to look like that as if I could ever replicate it, and she casually replied, "Oh, I don't do anything. My best friend Sarah, who owns a hair salon in New York, handles it." I'm quickly realizing she has someone for everything.

"Is that so?" she asks, locking her eyes with mine. It's been a while, but not long enough for me to hold her gaze for more than 30 seconds at a time. I look away quickly, but I don't need to see her to know she's already laughing.

"I'm serious!" My voice is a few octaves too high and noticeably louder than intended, and I wince while looking around at the sleeping passengers.

"I can tell, but you are comparing me to a man, which is pretty funny." She looks over my face before taking another sip and setting her glass down carefully. Every movement she makes is smooth, calculated, and confident. I can tell she doesn't doubt herself, she seems so sure of everything–the complete opposite of me.

For the remaining two hours of our 5-hour flight, I spent it completely out of my head and immersed in the moment. Not a single thought crossed my mind as we laughed and talked about nonsense. We didn't mention much about our personal lives which I'm grateful for. We still don't even know each other's names. It hadn't really crossed my mind until now, but I kind of like it that way.

After her first glass, we kept ordering more and more until we were soon cut off. But even then, she was so composed, and put together. Never telling me too much about her job or secret projects on her laptop. She really could be James Bond.

"I mean you're quiet, confident, mysteriou–"

"And handsome?" She interrupts. Her smirk grows into a grin while my face turns pink.

"I didn't mean it like that...I just meant you're a hard nut to crack." My words stumble over each other as I try to recover.

"Uh-huh," she says, and I have to stop myself from rolling my eyes. I really wish she'd stop saying that. Every time I say something even remotely risky, she stares blankly at me, letting the silence stretch out so long that I start to rethink my entire existence—only for her to finally say, "Uh huh." I know it's just the drinks, but somehow, I'm craving more from a complete stranger.

A while ago, I pulled out my Uno cards to distract her from reopening her laptop, which, much to her dismay, actually worked. But I instantly regretted it when I watched her take off her blazer to reveal a plain black, skin-tight short-sleeve top. It accentuates every curve of her body, and holy shit, her tattoos. Her arms are covered in ink—something I hadn't noticed before because of the blazer. The tattoos end just above her gold watch, which perfectly matches her rings and loafers.

I can hardly control my eyes as they widen to the size of saucers. Unsurprisingly, she's won every round—it seems to come to her with ease as if she doesn't even have to try. Meanwhile, I can't deny that I was clearly distracted.

"Ohhh, come onnnn!" I toss down my most recent hand of losing cards as she declares "Uno!" for the 5th or 6th time.

"You've got to be cheating."

She tilts her head to the side and raises one brow "Now, don't be a sore loser." She says it as a joke but the slight firmness of her tone and the small command makes the air catch in my throat, and I clear it before I fall deeper into my fantasy.

"I'm not, there's just no way you win 5 times in a row."

She's grinning again, I don't ever want her to stop.

"It was six actually, and I'm sorry you can't keep up." She replies. All I can do is scoff in response.

Before either of us can continue, the intercom above us interrupts abruptly, and the pilot's voice echoes through the plane. "Ladies and gentlemen, welcome to the Big Apple! We are going to be beginning our descent. Please be sure you are seated and your seatbelts are fastened. In addition, my crew will be making their last rounds for trash. Please stow away your trays and any personal belongings. Thank you for your patience."

And just like that, the flight attendants are heading down the aisle grabbing our glasses and miscellaneous trash. My smile from before is completely gone and replaced with a visible frown. I hadn't realized that we had been playing Uno for 2 hours, and by the looks of it, we were the only ones awake. All the passengers around us are just now sitting forward and gathering their belongings.

I glance over at her, and she's already looking back at me, expressionless. I'm not sure what I expected, but I knew this moment would end eventually, even though I kind of didn't want it to. I was definitely stepping further out of my comfort zone than I thought I would, but that's the whole point of this trip—and it was actually fun. Sure, I didn't really need to lie about my career, but what's one little lie? I'll never see her again, and I'm about to land in one of the biggest cities in the world.

By the time I finally come to my senses and fix my face, we're already landing. We mainly sit there in silence while we wait for our gate to open, and for the first time, I don't feel the rush or panic of everyone running to wait in the aisle. The passengers in first class look so calm, waiting patiently. I mean, I would too if I had complimentary champagne on every flight.

I glance over to see her thumbs typing quickly on her phone.

"Telling your husband you landed?" I ask. I'm not even tipsy anymore, these are completely sober mistakes that I have to live with.

Her head snaps up from her phone and does that same once-over of my face that sends chills down my spine. It makes me want to keep testing the waters like it's a game.

But my moment is ruined when everyone in front of us starts to stand up, meaning the doors are opening. I glance back at her, but she's already on her feet, retrieving her bag from the overhead compartment.

Great.

...

As we shuffled off the plane, squeezed in line with her right behind me, I could almost feel her breath on my neck—I nearly leaned back into the moment, lost in my imagination. Instead, I straightened up, made my way out of the gate, and focused on the signs above to find baggage claim. By the time I finally stepped off the plane, the mystery writer was already gone, and I never noticed which direction she bolted off to.

After waiting impatiently for my suitcase, I finally make it outside to the pickup area. Joey instructed me to catch a taxi to my hotel, where all of my accommodations are already arranged.

It's freezing, just as I expected, but I clutch Izzie's coat tightly against my chest to shield myself from the harsh winds. The sun is still shining brightly, forcing me to raise a hand to shield my eyes as I take in my surroundings. Finally, as my vision clears, I spot an older man in a long black coat holding a white sign that reads "SPEARS."

My eyes widen when I look past him and see the black SUV waiting behind him. There's only one Spears I know who was supposed to fly into New York today—maybe they sent a car to pick him up. Still in shock, I start walking toward him with my mouth gaping. Just as I'm about to speak, a familiar voice cuts through the wind like a whip, making my head snap around in response.

"You're Chef Spears?!"

It's the same mysterious girl from earlier, but she's walking towards me—fast. So much is happening at once that I don't even process the question until she's already standing in front of me, her hand extended for a handshake as if we've never met before.

"I'm Eden Turner, I'm the Editor that's writing your article for *Foodie*."

CHAPTER 7

Riley

"I'm sorry, what?!" I blurt out.

My brain is just now registering the past thirty seconds, and I still haven't even shaken her outstretched hand.

No.

No.

No.

This cannot be happening right now. My eyes are blinking rapidly and my chest is getting tight. Oh my god, am I dying?

Her hand drops but her smile widens. "Look, I'm just as surprised as you are. I'm used to interviewing egotistical, hyper-masculine, conceited men. But, I am pleasantly surprised. So I guess I'll be seeing you soon, right?"

I don't even realize I'm slowly backing away from her until I feel myself crash into something solid, and two hands grab my sides to stabilize me as I jerk forward.

"Oh my god, I'm so sorry," I gasp.

"Oh, it's no problem. It's a pleasure to meet you, Chef Spears. I'm Will, and I will be your driver for your entire trip. May I take your bags?" Both Will and Eden are looking at me with hopeful eyes. My head snaps back and forth between them as my mind races, and it feels like I could collapse at any moment. I should say something—I should confess. I'm not really Chef Spears. The truth is, I just make fruit displays for a living, and this whole thing has been one big lie. But when I look into Eden's eyes again, they have this look to them, it's not just hope. I can't tell what it is, but the mystery of her makes me respond quickly.

"Of course, I'll be there Monday morning!" I say. She smirks at my response, but I don't linger on it. I turn back to Will, who's already grabbed my bags and is holding the back door open with a bright smile. For a moment, I almost forget what I just did.

"Oh, thank you so much," I express my gratitude as he nods his head and shuts the door behind me. That's when I look out my window and realize Eden is still standing there–just watching. I'm thankful it's tinted to block my face. But it doesn't seem to matter because her eyes feel like they could break the window between us.

Even after Will rounds the car and starts driving, she's still standing there. But I can't focus on that right now—the weight of the past six hours is finally hitting me.

What the fuck did I just do?

What started as a simple, fun little lie has snowballed into what could be a shit show. Really it's my 'not so mysterious' girl's fault, she started this whole thing. If it weren't for her stupid shoes, long legs, expensive suit, curly hair, and that annoyingly calm expression, I wouldn't have felt the need to lie. But I thought I left all of that behind on the plane. But I didn't know I was doing all of this to a freaking editor. I knew she was hiding something, but the editor of *FOODIE*? I mean come on, how was I supposed to guess that would happen?

My mind won't stop racing through all of the points where I went wrong, I don't even take in the view of New York. What am I supposed to do now? I can't let this continue, I mean, I just lied to my driver for God's sake.

That thought makes me finally look up to see us pulling up in front of none other than The Ritz Hotel. There is no fucking way.

"We've arrived, Miss." My eyes meet Will's in his rearview mirror before getting out to open my door. My eyebrows are scrunched together but my eyes are wide. How is this possible? It's like life is playing some sick joke on me right now.

The gold awning with scalloped glass edges sits next to the navy blue and gold Ritz Hotel flag. It feels like a movie set—gold luggage carts lined up out front, and a bellman approaching so purposefully that I half expect a producer to pop out and call, "Action!"

"Chef Spears! We've been awaiting your arrival. All of your accommodations are in place, and your Itinerary is already waiting for you in your room. If you'd follow me this way please." I don't get a word in after he ushers me inside the hotel because he's already across the lobby guiding me to the elevators.

The floors are so shiny that you can see the beautiful chandelier hanging above in their reflection. Upholstered chairs fill the room, with art lining the walls in their huge gold frames all lit by dim lighting. I feel like I shouldn't be here, probably because I actually shouldn't.

I must be standing there gawking for too long, because the bellman, holding my luggage, is waiting with one hand propping open the elevator doors and the other waving me over.

I quickly make my way over to him, stepping onto the nicest elevator I've ever seen. I don't even see what floor he presses because I'm too busy taking in all of the details—every element, from the floors to the mirrors, was crafted with intention.

When we finally arrive at my room, I expect it to be beautiful given the location, but I'm not prepared for it to completely blow the lobby and elevator out of the water.

"Can I give you a tour?" he asks politely. I almost forget the bellman is holding the door open, but he seems more amused than annoyed.

After eagerly nodding my head, he shows me through every room. Yes, every room—this was the Executive Suite. He takes me to the main room first, where open seating includes a sofa facing the extraordinary view of Central Park. It's not that anything was flashy or overly bright; it was calm, neutral, and relaxing. The bathroom featured marble covering the floor and walls, double sinks, a walk-in shower, and a tub.

The bedroom is my favorite, though. It faces a huge window, giving you another view of Central Park. What should have been the smallest detail on this tour makes me freeze in my tracks–the bed. Its plain, white appearance looks comfortable, but all I can picture on it is Eden. I can't focus on anything but her, and that blank look she gives me that drives me insane.

I clear my throat to clear my thoughts and turn around to meet my tour guide back at my door.

"Your itinerary was left in the living area, please let us know if you need anything." Once again, he's down the hallway and back to the elevator before I can even say "Thank you."

But after closing the door and letting out a huge sigh because this is the first time I've had a moment alone since the disaster this morning. As I make my way to the living area I find the itinerary sheet, which luckily for me doesn't start until Monday, leaving me with the remainder of today and tomorrow to rest up.

I'm unsure how to navigate the situation since I've lied to everyone that I've met out here so far.

What catches my eye is the handwritten note at the bottom of the page that reads:

Thank you again for coming to New York to do your first article on Wendigo. We can't wait to hear and share your story! Hopefully, the room and driver are up to par! - The *Foodie* Team

This is just getting worse by the second, but I'm pulled out of my head when I hear my phone ringing from my back pocket. I grab it quickly and see Izzie trying to FaceTime me. Oh, thank God, someone who knows the *real* me. I couldn't answer it any faster.

"Finally! You were supposed to call when you land–WAIT! WHERE THE HELL ARE YOU? PRINCESS DIANA'S CASTLE?" Izzie shouts, trying to move her head as if she can peer around me through the screen. I flip the camera around to give her a tour while I try not to pee myself from laughing so hard. Midway through the call she adds Joshua so he can see too.

"Shit, you really *are* on vacation! Have you met anyone from *Foodie* yet?" Josh asks excitedly. Reality sadly strikes again, and I flip the camera back to my now frowning self. Compared to the marble walls I just showed them, the contrast is jarring.

"Oh, God. What happened?"

I contemplate not saying anything and just holding onto this embarrassment, but these two are the only people who truly understand me, I can't lie to them too. So, I take a deep breath before exhaling and start telling them the entire story, beginning with when I left this morning.

By the time I'm finished, they both are staring at me with wide eyes before bursting into laughter. All I can do is close my eyes in defeat.

Joshua is still laughing but he finally manages to say "Riley, what the actual fuck?!"

"I told you to go on a vacation, not get yourself into a bigger shit show than you're already in here," Izzie interjects. A few seconds of silence pass before she continues.

"But there's no point in pouting, you're just going to have to go with it." My head finally snaps up in confusion.

"What does that even mean? This isn't a game anymore! I have to cook for these people Iz, and I'm clearly not Chef Spears!" My voice is getting higher with how fast my heart is racing, this is all too much.

"Yes, but you *are* a Chef, Riley; you weren't wrong about that. Now you can use this as an opportunity to show your work, Riles. You've been screaming from the rooftops about how bad you want this chance. Well, here it is. You may not be Chef Spears, but you *are* Chef Bennett."

CHAPTER 8

Eden

"Heyy! Did you get any rest after your flight?" My eyes don't leave my laptop screen as I hear footsteps entering my home office.

"Not really." I didn't get any sleep last night, actually. The smell of freshly roasted coffee hits my nose and I look up to see Kat, my assistant, sliding a hot mug across my desk. I visibly sigh and finally let my shoulders drop.

"Oh my god, you're a lifesaver," I say, not even waiting for her response before closing my eyes to savor my first sip of heaven and pure bliss.

"I know, and it looks like you need it, crappy flight?" The question makes my head snap up, but I don't reply. I don't really know what to say, because that is precisely the reason I couldn't sleep last night. Every time I tried to close my eyes I would get flashes of her blonde hair, or I could hear her tipsy giggles replaying like a track on a loop. Even the feeling of her eyes burning holes into the side of my skull as I worked, just made my jaw clench. I could barely finish the project I was supposed to do on the flight home, but when she ordered me a drink, I gave in.

Kat is looking back at me with raised eyebrows. She's been my assistant and best friend for the past 4 years. Ever since I started at *Foodie* she's been my right hand and partner in crime. She books all my flights, arranges my meetings, and knows what I'm supposed to be doing almost every second of the day. So when something's off, she knows. There's no point in hiding it.

"I wouldn't say crappy...just interesting. I couldn't get much work done."

"Eden Turner not getting work done? How is that possible? What was the distraction?" She's already pulling the chair in front of me closer, clearly eager to find out.

"Well, I met Chef Spears." I meet her eyes to see they've doubled in size.

"What?! He was on your flight? How is that possible?!" She's spitting out the questions like rapid fire, and I raise my mug to take another sip before dropping the real bomb.

"Don't know, but the bigger shock was when I found out *he* was actually a *she*, and that we were seated right next to each other..." My eyebrows raise, lips tight, as her jaw drops.

"No fucking way!" I simply nod in response. We sit in silence for a moment, and when she finally speaks again I almost choke on my coffee.

"Well, was she hot?" she demands, leaning forward eagerly.

"*That's* what you want to know?" I challenge, barely containing my frustration. Kat is practically on the edge of her seat at this point.

"Well, was she?" She never fails to push my buttons. And I can't just say she was the most beautiful girl I've ever seen. Or how the image of her on the floor looking up at me is ingrained in my memory.

"Well, she fell right in front of me so I didn't get much of a look at her." I shrug my shoulders and begin typing, hoping that will end this conversation faster. I can't take any more questions.

"Righhhhht. You sat through a five-hour flight not looking at the hot chef sitting right next to you?" My fingers stop typing, hovering above the keyboard, I guess that *does* sound crazy.

"I mean, we talked, not about much. When she told me she was a chef I didn't think much of it until I saw her heading to a driver that was holding a sign with the name 'Spears' on it." Which is true; I did try to keep to myself for most of the flight because that's what I'm used to. I like to spend my time in the clouds doing what I love–writing.

So as you can imagine my frustration was on the rise when she wouldn't stop moving next to me. It was like she *wanted* me to stop working. At a certain point, I had to physically stop myself from grabbing her thigh. That's unlike me, I can work through anything. Someone snoring as loud as an engine or a baby crying their life away, I'm always able to get my work done. Kat knows this too, that's why she is squinting her eyes, trying to read me. She knows I am not telling her something, but I refuse to give her anything else.

"Hmm, well, we'll all just have to see for ourselves on Monday," referencing the rest of our team/friend group. She gives me this knowing smirk like this is far from being over.

"Kat, please don't make this into anything bigger than it needs to be. It's just like any other article, okay?" and even though I know I'm lying, I cock my head to the side to give her my 'don't start' look.

"Oh, come onnnn, this is the first chef from Vegas that we are interviewing–who's a woman, and you're telling me this is like any other article?" That question makes me feel stupid–I should be happy I'm not stuck with another dickhead of a chef mansplaining everything to me. But did it have to be *her*? I don't have time for sleepless nights or Kat investigating my personal life.

"Just keep it professional, okay?" But by the time I look up for a response, Kat's already out of my office, probably already texting the others. My head drops into my hands letting out a much-needed breath. Fuck, I really need to take my house key back from her.

...

I spent the rest of Sunday finishing up the work I didn't get done on my flight. An article on a new restaurant opening up in Las Vegas, it's a Circus-themed restaurant. When I visited this past week, I was able to witness acrobats flying in the air and trapeze artists walking overhead as we ate. It was both as beautiful and as hectic as it sounds. I was so stressed that someone was going to fly into my food that I could barely focus. And even when I got the moment to really take in my food, it was mediocre. Braised chicken over asparagus and a cauliflower mash. Sounds amazing, but it was cold to the touch, dry, and overall underwhelming.

Yes, our reviews can seem a bit harsh, but when you are talking about Vegas we're talking about extravagant shows and extravagant dinners, *not* one or the other. People travel all across the world to see what Vegas has to offer, and repeatedly–I'm disappointed. You're better off flying in and grabbing In-N-Out before your show. But the last time I said that in an article the chef called me a "dumb know-it-all whore from New York," and even though we all couldn't stop laughing for weeks, we had to reel it in.

So here I am on a Sunday evening writing about how "If you want something simple with an incredible show then *The Flying Plate* is the perfect restaurant to book for your time in Vegas." It's the nicest thing I can think of without flat-out saying "BORING."

After I press *send* to Jay, who does my proofing, I finally close my laptop. I knew it had to be late due to the darkness consuming the glass windows behind me. But I'm still shocked when I pick up my phone for the first time in hours and finally look at the clock, which reads 8:50 p.m.

Great. I'm supposed to be asleep in two hours and by the looks of it, this is going to be another long night of tossing and turning.

...

Riley

All I've done since getting off the phone with Joshua and Iz is pace, and obsessively research Eden Turner and all of her work. I didn't get a second of sleep.

How could I?

Their pep talk was great, but the high only lasted for about 30 minutes until I dug into Eden's work. Shit, she's tough. She doesn't seem like the type to have time for average meals, (or fake chefs that have no idea what the hell they're doing.) I anxiously read over a review she did on a restaurant called *Blank Space,* a pitch-black dining experience in Vegas that opened around a year ago. I still haven't even gotten a reservation there, they're booked out for the next 2 years.

"You would think my other senses would be heightened when losing my sight of the dishes, but the brown butter and thyme scallops were just as dull and dim as the lighting." It just kept going. I read article after article, and with each one, I gained a better understanding as to why this was such a big deal. I could tell by the first-class flight, stunning hotel, and everything else *Foodie* was doing for Spears, that this *had* to be big. But the pressure to impress is through the roof.

I don't have time to panic anymore. After my investigation into Eden, I fell asleep on the sofa with my laptop open. Even when I woke up in the middle of the night I couldn't bring myself to go to bed because all I could think about was her, and I was already doing enough of that.

So when I finally woke up, I spent all Sunday devising a game plan to get through the week as quickly as possible, without fucking things over for Spears and the whole Wendigo team. This reflects everyone, and they're counting on me to kill it.

I started by going through the itinerary for Monday. If I break down the recipes I'll be cooking in their test kitchen day by day, maybe it'll be an easier pill to swallow.

MONDAY:

6:00 A.M. — Hotel pick-up, meet the team, and tour the Test Kitchen!

7:00 A.M. — Recipe Trial #1 (Something light and fresh to start!)

10:00 A.M. — Photos

11:00 A.M. — Taste test and interview

12:00 P.M. — Driver will arrive for pick-up

"Light and fresh." Okay, I can do that. I immediately start brainstorming, and for hours my mind races from idea to idea. I considered stuffed duck with garden-roasted veggies, but that's too basic. Then I had the idea to do Chef Spears' habanero caramelized shrimp over a bed of corn salsa, but I don't think it's what they're looking for.

By 10 p.m., I catch myself dozing off on the couch again, clearly avoiding the bed. But as my eyes start to close for the night, I come up with the perfect recipe and finally manage to fall into a deep sleep.

CHAPTER 9

Riley

I don't realize someone's at my door until the fourth or fifth knock, and even then, I can barely pry myself off the couch. But as soon as my feet touch the plush rug my eyes spring open. I'm not in my small apartment in Vegas, and judging by how bright it is outside and the persistent knocking, I don't even have to guess– I've overslept.

Oh my god, how could I do this? I planned everything out down to a T, but I forgot to set a stupid alarm?!

I scramble to grab my phone, lodged between the couch cushions, and check the time, 5:45 A.M. Fuck, I have to be at the *Foodie* Test Kitchen in less than twenty minutes. The sixth knock on my door snaps me out of my thoughts, and I nearly trip over my feet running to answer it. I don't even bother fixing my hair before yanking the door open, only to find a surprised Will, his fist still raised to knock.

"Oh, I'm so sorry Chef Spears, I don't mean to scare you but I do think we should head out now. I don't want you to be late." There's not a hint of judgment in his eyes, just pure concern that amplifies the anxiety attack that's already brewing.

"Yes, yes, of course! I'm so, so sorry to keep you waiting. I promise I will be just a few minutes." Before he can respond, I'm running in the opposite direction, letting the door close behind me.

My time in culinary school finally pays off when I pull my hair back into the sleek low bun with a middle part that I used to do almost every day. It's second nature now, so it takes less than two minutes. I shouldn't smell bad since I showered yesterday, but just in case, I throw on some deodorant. Luckily, I already had my dove-gray chef coat picked out and ironed.

Within ten minutes, I'm running through the Ritz lobby to meet Will, who's standing just as he was at the airport, holding my door open. I slide in swiftly, squeezing out a "Thank you!" while catching my breath before Will closes my door and runs around the SUV to the driver's door

I spend the rest of the drive gripping the edge of my seat and leaning forward as if I'm trying to make the car go faster. My head is whipping all around, taking in the surroundings that I missed on the drive from the airport. And for a moment, everything leaves my brain. This is incredible. The buildings in Vegas are nothing compared to these skyscrapers. Looking up, I can only imagine the views from the top.

My attention snaps back to the street when Will honks at someone trying to cut us off. He slams on the gas, and the sudden jolt sends me crashing back into my seat.

He then meets my eyes in the rearview mirror. "Sorry Chef, but I guess this is the best way to welcome you to New York–the place where you have to know your destination and be aggressive about it." That makes me laugh. Even though this morning turned into a mess because of me, I can't help but smile, taking in the fact that I'm actually here. Even if I'm not actually myself, today and for the rest of the week, I am Chef Spears.

After giving myself a mini pep talk to help calm my nerves, we finally arrive at a huge warehouse-style building. It's completely made of red brick, and even from the backseat of the car, I can see the massive windows stretching across the entire upper half of the building. I barely have a moment to take it all in before Will is out of the car, opening my door.

I look up to see a woman with brown hair and heels, running out of the building toward me, her smile wide and full of excitement.

"Chef Spears!" she exclaims. It takes me a moment to remember that's me, but she's already standing right in front of me.

"It's so nice to meet you in person, I'm Kat. I'm the one who's been trying to set this interview up for a while. I'm so sorry for all the back and forth over email. You know how stressful these things can get, right?" Her eager smile makes me think quickly on my feet.

"Yeah, of course. I understand. I'm so sorry for being late! It was completely all my fault." Her brows furrowed with confusion before looking down at her watch.

"Oh, please, it's only 6:20, everyone's late on Mondays!" Her welcoming energy makes me visibly relax and we both laugh.

"We should head in though, I really want to get you introduced to everyone, and give you a tour of our space!" She's already grabbing my arm and pulling me while I turn to say "Thank you" and goodbye to Will. As usual, he offers me a soft smile and a quick nod.

As soon as we head into the building, we're met with a security guard who doesn't even bat an eye as Kat ushers me through the lobby and into the biggest elevator I've ever stepped foot in. It looks like the type of elevator used to transfer large furniture or equipment. My concern must be obvious because Kat starts laughing.

"It's called a freight elevator, it makes deliveries so much easier." As the elevator doors close, she pulls down the gate and presses the buttons. Even if I wanted to run away, I'm shit out of luck now.

"What kind of building was this?" I ask, my curiosity getting the better of me.

"It used to be an old printing factory, but around three years ago *Foodie* was expanding insanely fast, due to Eden, of course. We needed a new space–quick. So, Eden had this insane idea to transform this industrial-style space into a studio-style Test Kitchen." My eyebrows immediately shoot up realizing all of this is Eden's work.

"Everyone thought she was insane, myself included. But she wanted to go all in, so we did, and now we have this..."

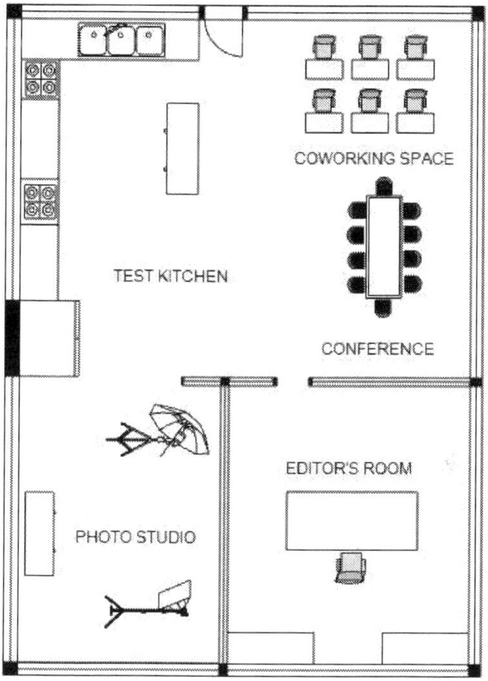
COWORKING SPACE
TEST KITCHEN
CONFERENCE
EDITOR'S ROOM
PHOTO STUDIO

The elevator doors open and Kat is pulling up the gate to reveal what feels like every chef's dream. As soon as I walk in, I look to the right to see endless stainless steel. It's gorgeous. I can't help myself from stepping in further not even noticing Kat behind me.

"It's all custom made, Eden designed it to be perfect for any chef to be able to come in and make any recipe needed." I make my way around the steel prep table to the matching cabinets and huge three-compartment sink. Not to mention the amount of kitchen appliances along the counters that look practically brand new. A dehydrator, food processor, pressure cooker, and even a full-size freeze dryer.

I turn back to Kat who hasn't stopped smiling, "This is insane, how is this place even real?!" She just giggles in response.

"Geez, it's so nice to hear someone *actually* appreciate the space that she worked so hard to create. We're all so used to men coming in here and acting like our space is nothing compared to their restaurant." I'm even more shocked now. Just looking around, I can tell that half the equipment they have here is stuff we couldn't even dream of having at Wendigo.

When I turn back to respond, I finally notice the rows of office desks and chairs behind Kat, nearly all filled with people typing away at lightning speed. They seem completely unbothered by my presence.

"Team, this is Chef Spears. Chef Spears, this is our editing and research team." As I start to wave at everyone smiling at me, it suddenly hits me just how real this is.

This is a legit team of people ready to see what I'm going to create. "And if we head this way–" Kat is already across the room moving on, "–to the left, is where we have our team meetings every day." Hmm, just like back home, except the conference table where they have their meetings is probably bigger than the entire kitchen at Wendigo.

"That's Eden's office, and opposite it is our photography studio where you'll be working with Rach. So right after cooking, you can go straight into taking pictures without wasting any time. The space was designed to make everything accessible for ev—"

I realize I should pay attention to every word Kat says; I don't have the luxury of daydreaming right now. I really need to be present.

But as soon as she pointed toward Eden's office, everything else went in one ear and out the other. It's in the corner of the building, diagonally across from the kitchen. Even though I can't see inside because of the blackout glass, I have a feeling she can see out, meaning she can watch every second of me cooking without me knowing. Something about that makes the hair on my arms and neck stand on end. Just as my thoughts start to darken, Kat pulls me out of my head by walking away and yelling.

"Hey! Speak of the devil, I was just finishing the tour!" My head snaps back to the elevator doors to see Eden standing completely still. Her curls are pulled back into a clip, and she's wearing an all-black suit similar to the one I saw her in when we first met. Which makes me wonder if this is a thing of hers. She's also holding a briefcase in one hand and what looks like a coffee in the other.

It feels like hours pass before I finally manage to speak up "Hey! It's nice to see you again!" It's possible my voice is *slightly* higher than it needs to be. She simply glances past me at something on the wall, then looks back at me with an arched eyebrow.

"Really? 'Cause you're late." My mouth is gaping open and I can feel the eyes on me as my body temperature starts to rise.

I clear my throat and adjust my stance. "I'm so sorry, it's completely my fault I just let the time get away from me." I can barely look at her, so I glance over at Kat with pleading eyes but she's already glaring at Eden.

"Look who's talking? Didn't you just walk in?" she questions. Eden looks away and I can finally take a breath.

"Just let me know when it's time for the review, okay?" Eden says looking at Kat like she wants to rip her head off. I don't think I'll ever understand their dynamic, but I'm beyond grateful for Kat's presence.

Eden doesn't spare me another glance as she walks past me, straight to her office in the back, hearing the door close behind her.

"Don't worry about her, okay? She's a bitch every day, but Mondays just make her extra bitchy sometimes." We both laugh as she puts a hand on my shoulder, guiding me back to the kitchen.

"Okay, every ingredient you can think of can be found in the fridge, freezer, and those dry rack shelves. If there's anything you're missing, just let me know and I will get Meg, our personal shopper, on it." I can't tell if I'm overwhelmed, scared, excited, or all of the above. I turn to Kat to give her a soft smile and say, "Thank you" and she's gone.

Leaving me to create anything my heart desires. I have four hours to cook, and I need every second of it. After standing in the kitchen like a Sim character, I finally gather my thoughts and remember my plan. I start by gathering my ingredients and familiarizing myself with the kitchen, locating all the necessary appliances. The kitchen is so expansive that it's easy to get lost in it, but having all this space to myself feels like a blessing. I begin to find my groove while prepping, and by the one-hour mark, I'm completely in the zone. I don't even notice the time passing until I'm plating up. Finally, I look up and see the clock reads 9:30 AM. Perfect—I'm done early, even with being late.

My mind is so scattered that the photography session passes in a blur. Rachel, who is the absolute sweetest, adjusts the lighting, positioning, and everything else to capture the perfect shot. When she shows me the results, I'm left speechless.

"Pretty good, huh?" Rachel asks, scrolling through the images on her camera, and I can't stop shaking my head.

"No, you're a magician," I say, and she bursts out laughing.

"I wouldn't say that. This is all you! Are you ready to show Eden?" And with that question, I'm back to reality–Eden. Saying "no" isn't an option and if I overthink it more than I already am, I'll just run right out of here. I simply sigh and pick up my plate, heading to her office door.

I knock three times, silently praying she evaporated from her office and isn't actually here. But I'm sadly mistaken when I hear her say "Come in!" and even then, I want to act like I didn't hear her. Instead, I close my eyes, letting out another breath before finally entering.

I try not to let my eyes wander, but I can't help it. I take a quick once-over at what seems to be the most fitting office for Eden.

Everything is either black or gray, two matching bookcases frame the space. The desk is clearly the centerpiece. It's massive and made entirely of concrete, just like the floors. Everything else is a blur.

When my gaze finally meets Eden, she's seated at her desk, already looking back at me with that same unreadable expression, waiting for me to speak.

"Umm, I just finished up with Rachel, so I thought you might be ready for a taste test?" I prompt, shakily. She doesn't respond; she merely points to her desk, signaling me to set the plate down.

As I make my way over, I trip slightly and nearly drop the plate. Fortunately, Eden saves the day by catching it with one hand and placing it carefully between us. Though I can't fully decipher her expression, I notice her eyebrows lift in surprise.

"You made me a fruit salad?"

CHAPTER 10

Eden

"Yes! It's made with dragon fruit, dark cherries, strawberries, blackberries, and blueberries. I also made a sour Tanghulu sugar-coating for you to break through."

My eyes are blinking rapidly, attempting to register what I'm looking at. The fruit has an almost cartoon-like shine to it, which I'm assuming is from the hard sugar coating. You can turn the plate in any direction without seeing any movement.

When I was watching her earlier, I definitely didn't think *this* was what she was working so hard on. There were so many moments when I wanted to go over and ask her questions, but after Kat stormed into my office to yell at me, I figured it was best to stay put. Granted, I haven't been in the best mood since I got zero sleep the night before, and it didn't help that the first person I saw today was the one who kept me up all night. So I snapped, and I most definitely deserved it when Kat came and said the rest of the office doesn't deserve my shitty energy.

So I waited and waited, *and* waited. Finally, I watched her leave the photography studio to come to my office. When she knocked, I had to act like I wasn't just sitting there, watching her every move.

But now, I'm tempted to let it all out. How is it that, after watching her run around for three hours, searching for everything and using damn near every appliance we have, this is what I'm reviewing—a fruit salad? I've been quiet for a while, but I just can't seem to find the words. "Uhh–" I finally look up to see an obviously nervous Chef Spears, holding out a spoon for me to take.

"If you want, you can use this spoon to break the shell first." I can tell she's intentionally not making eye contact. Shit, am I that scary?

I take the spoon, barely grazing her hand, and we both jump from a jolt that feels like an electric shock. I brush it off and start hitting the surprisingly hard exterior of the shell. By the time I finally break through, I realize I'm smiling. When I look up, her expression mirrors mine.

Without speaking, I look down to take my first bite of the perfectly sculpted dragon fruit spheres and bits of blackberries. With one bite, it hits me–every step she's taken in the past 3 hours was deliberate. The satisfying snap of the shell makes me close my eyes to savor the moment. The bright flavors of dragon fruit and blackberries blend with a tangy green apple taste, creating a party in my mouth. "Where's the sourness coming from?" I ask. I'm still staring down at the plate as if it isn't real, it can't be.

"Umm, it's citric acid. Is it okay?" Her confused eyes make me scoff and shake my head.

"I mean, this is incredible. I've never had anything like it" Her eyebrows shoot up, and the smile growing on her face makes me continue. "–the citric acid mixing with the natural sugars from the fruit makes it like a deconstructed piece of candy."

"Really?!" Her eyes are now bigger than when she fell in front of me on the plane.

"It's genius, really." All I can do is look at her in awe. I've never once called any chef who entered the *Foodie* Test Kitchen "genius." I'd rather eat rat poop than ever give them that big of an ego boost. Seeing Spears' face light up as if I've just fulfilled all her dreams reminds me that this isn't like any other article. We're only one recipe in, and she's already blowing my mind. If this is how it's going to be, I really can't be trusted to stay objective.

"Oh wow, thank you so much!" she beams. God, it's getting hot in here–fast. I really need to go. I begin speaking quickly, attempting to mask how awkward I feel.

"Mhmm. Well, I'm actually going to have Kat do the interview today because I have a meeting to get to. If you can ask Rach to get some more photos of it shattered, that'd be amazing to include for the article." I'm already on my feet, moving toward the office door and holding it open for her to pass through.

"Oh, okay. Of course, thank you again!" she says quickly.

I don't respond. Instead, I close the door behind her and lean against it, frustration boiling over. Fuck me, how the hell is this going to work if I have to make up a lie to get out of doing my own job?

I grab my briefcase and my nearly empty coffee cup, then rush for the elevator. As soon as I step inside, I make the mistake of glancing up and spotting Kat, Rach, and Spears working together in the photography studio. Kat's knowing, almost sinister gaze makes me hit the buttons quickly, trying to avoid the inevitable conversation I know is coming.

...

Riley

Holy shit, I did it.

I actually did it.

I haven't had much time to really think about anything. Everything happened so fast, When Eden was trying my food it felt like some type of sick joke. I never expected that seeing someone eat something I made would overwhelm me this much. When she asked about the ingredients, I was so distracted that I couldn't think straight. I've never had anyone react to my food as if it actually mattered before. Besides Josh and Izzie, no one has really complimented my work in years.

So even after Eden told me she couldn't stay, I couldn't really pout for long when I reminded myself what I accomplished. When Rach started taking more pictures I couldn't help but smile thinking about my work being mentioned in a real article.

"Seems like you had a great day. This article for Wendigo is going to be insane. I don't think we've done one like this!" Kat throws me a wink over her shoulder before helping to readjust the position of the plate.

Fuck. Wendigo.

The thought of Chef Spears waking up to see a bowl of fruit under the headline of his article makes my eyes go wide. But it's far too late to go back now.

Once we finish up with the photos, Kat asks me a few questions for the article before walking me to the elevator. I can't help but feel a bit disappointed that Eden isn't here, but I make sure not to let it show. Today was so successful, that I can't let one interview out of however many bring me down, especially when I did so well.

"I'll see you tomorrow, right?" Kat asked cheerfully after I finished my rounds of saying goodbye and "Thank you" to everyone.

"Of course! Today was great." I reply. "You and everyone else here are seriously a dream to work with."

She smiles as she replies, "Well, you make our jobs really easy."

And with one swift motion, she's closing the gate to the elevator to send me down to meet Will, who is perfectly on time, standing outside the SUV.

"Heyyy, Will! How are ya'?" I nearly shout. He's already opening my door before I make my way over to him.

"I'm well, Chef Spears. Thank you for asking. Did everything go okay?" His sparse brows raise up so high it makes my heart swell. How can so many people be so caring and not even know who I am?

"Amazing, actually." We're both cheesing at each other, as I slide into my seat.

"I'm happy to hear that Miss, should I take you back to your hotel?" A spark hits me, suddenly, remembering I haven't decided on my dish for tomorrow.

"Can you take me to your favorite spot for some cozy food in the city, instead?" I ask, hoping he will go along with it.

His head tilts to the side in disbelief. "Are you sure you don't want me to make you a reservation at a restaurant in the Ritz?"

"No, I want your *real* opinion on the best comfort food in New York, nothing fancy, just your pick!" He looks at me for a moment before nodding his head while smiling, almost as if he's impressed.

"Well, you're in for a drive tonight, Miss." And he closes my door, leaving me to wonder what he has in store.

...

By the time Will says we've made it, I've gone through my entire day in my head–twice, already recognizing my mistakes and where I know I can do better. I also spent some time silently screaming at the fact that I not only did it, but I *killed* it today. Making fruit salads is definitely more fun when you're making them completely by yourself in a fully stocked, spaceship-like kitchen. I can't remember the last time I had this much fun cooking. Not a single grunt from a chef peering over your shoulders, telling you every move you make is "stupid." Just pure peace. Even Kat stayed to herself. It was like everyone was in their own world, completely focused.

And right now I'm focused on the fact that Will has me standing outside of a restaurant called "Katz." He told me it was best if I waited in the car but I couldn't help but step out when I saw the long line wrapped around the building. Holy shit, this place must be a gem.

The way he walked right past everyone and came back out with a crumpled, greasy brown bag in under five minutes made it clear he was a regular.

"I thought I told you to wait inside?" His look of concern makes me giggle.

"You thought I could sit still for almost an hour without needing to get out?" I challenge. The sound of my back cracking makes Will scrunch up his face as he opens my door.

"Understandable." He closes my door and hops into the front seat, turning around with a huge grin on his face.

"Okay, now this is what I would call a New York classic. This is as cozy and comforting as it gets."

My eyes are wide, and I'm on the edge of my seat, nearly shaking with hunger. Maybe it's because all I've had today are scraps of fruit from my sculpture, and it's finally catching up to me. But when Wills pulls out the thickest pastrami sandwich I've ever seen, drool nearly falls from my mouth. For the next fifteen minutes, we sit silently, stuffing our faces. Even if I had something to say, I wouldn't want to stop eating.

"Holy shit. Will, what the fuck was that?" I blurt out, finally breaking the silence. My chef coat is almost all the way open revealing my black undershirt that is also starting to feel constricting on my bloated stomach.

"I told you—a classic. Was it what you wanted when you said 'cozy'?" His brows are raised looking at me through the rearview mirror, already knowing the answer. But I'm so stuffed, all I can do is nod my head and lean on the door as Will laughs and begins the drive back to the hotel.

...

I barely make it to the couch before ripping my shoes off and dropping face-first onto the cushions. Before I fully relax, I pull out my phone to search for the loudest ringtone I can find and set an alarm for 5 a.m. I refuse to make that same mistake again, no matter how full I am.

As I slowly start to drift into a pastrami-induced dreamland, for the first time on this trip, I actually feel prepared and inspired.

CHAPTER 11

Riley

"Fuck. How many of those did you make?"

For the first time today, I finally look up to a wide-eyed Kat–who's practically panting over my finished product. I definitely took longer to cook today than I did yesterday, but when I finally set down the mini tongs I use for plating, every muscle in my body relaxes. I can feel the stress of the past 4 hours pour off my shoulders.

Luckily, this morning went as smooth as butter. I woke up before my alarm and arrived at the *Foodie* Test Kitchen with ten minutes to spare.

Unfortunately, I haven't seen Eden all morning so she hasn't seen anything. But the creative energy was flowing to me with ease so I ran with it. I didn't think too much, and just let my inspiration speak for itself. And with how Kat is looking at my plate full of mini pastrami sliders, I couldn't be happier.

"Umm...I don't know specifically, but definitely more than enough for pictures" I reply shyly.

"Would you say enough for a team of six?" She asks hopefully. Now I can see what she's thinking.

"Probably, why?" I reply with a smirk and she slowly breaks into a grin.

"Ugh, you're the best! Lunch is on Chef Spears today y'all!" The sudden roar of cheers coming from the team makes my smile match hers.

"Get some pics done first before everyone runs over here like madmen," she says with a wink before quickly walking away. I'm figuring out that Kat doesn't wait for anybody–not a reply, an answer, or anything. Once she's got what she needs–she's gone.I love ixt.

I make my way over to Rach who's been busy adjusting the light in the studio. Yesterday, she taught me how every angle matters.

I thought the pictures of my fruit salad were coming out great until she turned on another box light, and suddenly all of the pictures from before seemed so dull. It just makes me appreciate everyone's role here that much more.

"Hey! I'm all done and ready for some pics when you are!" I call out. Rachel's on her knees with her back towards me when I come in, but she whips around quickly.

"Hey! I was just getting the lighting right. I heard we were doing something 'cozy' so I thought we could go with a more warm setting!"

"I mean, I don't understand much of that but it sounds great!" I reply with a smile. We both laugh before I set the plate down on the white backdrop.

"Shit, those look amazing!"

The pastrami stack on each slider towers over the homemade brioche buns. As soon as I got to the Test Kitchen, I immediately started making the bread. It took an hour to rise and almost an hour to bake, but when I saw how fluffy and pillowy soft they turned out, I knew it was worth it. Against the juicy slices of pastrami hanging over the edges of the buns, the whole thing looks unreal.

"Yeah, I guess they do," I almost whisper. But Rach is already snapping away. I love watching her work; it's incredible to see the lengths she'll go to get the perfect shot. One second she's standing on a ladder to get an aerial view, and the next, she's down low, making the tiny slider look huge.

By the time she finishes, it is 11 a.m., when Eden is supposed to do my interview and taste test. But I still haven't seen her at all today, and Kat never told me she wasn't coming in. Granted, I never asked. She already missed the interview yesterday and now today. I'm starting to think *I'm* the problem.

But all of that is forgotten when I start to make my way from the photography studio back to the kitchen, and I see Kat is already waving me down. "Hey, I was just about to bring everyone over to the conference table to eat."

"Perfect, let me grab the extras from the warmer and I'll meet you over there," I reply.

And within seconds of me setting the sheet pan down on the table, it is completely cleared. All you could hear was moans and groans coming from all around the table. And all I could do was stare in awe. I've never had so many people so enamored by my work. *This* is why chefs act the way they do. I swear I could live off this high forever.

"This is insane, no one has ever made enough for all of us to try." Ty, one of the editors finally speaks up through a mouth full of food.

"No seriously, you are something else, Chef Spears!" Kat's words are so sincere I try not to let the mention of Spears spoil this moment for me.

But the moment ends abruptly when I hear the creak of a door opening behind me. I freeze. Everyone who should be here is right in front of me. When I look up, I see Kat smirking past me with a mischievous, amused expression. I know she can only be looking at one person. My throat tightens, the air suddenly feels thick, and my palms start to sweat like I'm about to present a project to a class.

"What the hell, Kat?" the voice cuts through the room. I can't sit still any longer, but I turn so fast that I almost fall out of my chair.

"You were supposed to let me know when everything was done! Are you *eating* the food?!" Eden demands. I can see her eyes narrowing down on everyone's plates, and she doesn't even take a breath before continuing.

"Have we even taken photos?!" She barks. Everyone's heads turn to Kat, she's still smirking, eyes fixed on Eden.

"Well, you would know if you came out of your dungeon at some point, now wouldn't you?" I can see the smoke ready to come out of Eden's ears, but no one else seems concerned. They're all still too busy eating, and some have started laughing. I can't seem to decide what to do. I had no idea Eden was even here. That means she could've seen me at any moment today. So many questions start to run through my head at a rapid speed.

How long has she been here for?

Did she see me trip when I was grabbing the pastrami from the fridge?

Has she seen the food already?

Was she watching when I went over to Rachel for pictures?

"Sorry Boss! Had no idea you were even here!" Ty says mid bite not even looking up to see Eden rolling her eyes.

Kat gives her a "See, I told you so" look.

"Seriously, Kat? I don't have time for this. I needed this interview done today." Her face drops along with her shoulders.

"And it *is* done. We had the best taste testers in the building try it, and they've already given Chef Spears rave reviews. Maybe next time, if you want to be a part of the taste test–try talking to the chef first?" Kat replies, unfazed.

That makes me turn back around completely and sink into my chair. Kat *knew* Eden was here. One part of me should be satisfied that Eden is getting called out for not doing her job, but the other part of me wants to run and hide. Am I really that bad? Am I *that* unbearable to be around?

It wasn't like this when we met on the plane. We were comfortable with each other, laughing like we had booked the flight together. But that was before she found out we'd be working together. Maybe she doesn't want those two worlds to mix. I can tell she's serious about her work and doesn't care for distractions.

I don't hear what Eden says in response, but I can tell Kat is not done with her.

"And don't say you can't be here tomorrow," she snaps.

I don't waste a second turning to see how Eden will respond, but I instantly regret it. She's already looking at me like she's weighing her options. Maybe it's because my back is to Kat and the others, so no one can see my face. I decide to take a chance, shifting my expression from one of desperation to a challenging look, raising an eyebrow as if to say, "Well, what are you going to do?" Eden stares at me for a moment, tilting her head and squinting, clearly taken aback by my audacity. When she finally responds, she doesn't even glance at Kat.

"No, I have a few bulk food items that I need to restock on." She finally turns back to Kat, but I cut her off before she can begin to yell again.

"I can go with you!" I exclaim.

Deja vu hits me like a ton of bricks when Eden's head snaps to me in confusion just like Chef Spears' did. I look over at Kat, who is just as shocked that I even spoke up.

"I mean, I'm just... uh, missing a few ingredients, so I thought I could go with you," I stammer.

Kats's face immediately switches back to grinning while Eden's remains the same. She is still watching me trying to figure out my game. "Absolutely not. We don't really do buddy shopping trips. Besides, we have a personal shopper!" Her words are stumbling over themselves, and for the first time, I can hear Eden Turner actually starting to panic.

I still don't acknowledge Eden's eyes on me as Kat begins to talk. "No, that's perfect! She can't cook without the ingredients, and you can spend the drive asking Chef Spears about her insane pastrami sliders that you didn't get to try!"

At this point, both Kat and I are giggling, while Eden remains silent, probably glaring daggers at me.

I'd prefer not to face her after pressuring her into spending the day with me in front of her whole team, who seem to be thoroughly enjoying the free entertainment, judging by their expressions.

"And you can pick her up from her hotel!" Kat adds, with an almost villainous smile.

A moment passes before I hear Eden's feet shift, "Great." Her voice is short and tight. I can feel the tension like a rubber band about to snap.

Kat turns to me with a softer smile and raises her brows.

I return her smile, "Great!"

CHAPTER 12

Riley

Just like when I was talking to Chef Spears, I don't know what possessed me to open my mouth and say, "I can go!" But unlike last time, this time I actually have to go with Eden. Since waking up at 4 a.m., I've spent the past hour pacing back and forth, running through all the worst-case scenarios for today. I could have let her go alone and avoided this stress. She clearly didn't want me to come, but something about her panic when I offered made me push harder.

And the way Kat was acting yesterday, tells me she sees it too. Eden's avoiding me, and whenever I'm near her it's like the tension and the heat in the room always begin to rise. Once it gets to a certain point it's too much for her, and she backs away from the fight. But yesterday, I felt oddly empowered when she didn't take my bait, yet I still pushed until it was impossible for her to say no. It was as if, for once, I was in control of the situation.

Ever since our plane ride, Eden has made it very clear that it was a fun moment that was never going to go any further. I mean, we haven't even spoken about our fight once. We haven't really spoken much at all. It seems like that's pretty uncommon for her when she's working with other chefs. If Kat has to call her out for avoiding me in front of everyone, then *something* isn't right here.

She's held the reins since we've met and now it's time for me to have some fun.

So, at 6 a.m., when I make it to the downstairs lobby of the Ritz and see Eden Turner herself in yet another black suit, I decide it's time to drop the work side of this trip for just a few hours.

"You really are serious about that suit, huh?"

By the time I reach her, her face is buried in her phone, but her eyes snap up the moment she hears my voice. She doesn't respond; she just scans me over, like she always does.

"You're wearing your chef coat?" I can't help but giggle at her quick response.

"Touché," I reply.

With that, she's already walking away, and out of the building. I can barely catch up. Her stride is twice the length of mine.

"Shit, is this how it's going to be all day? Are we in a race?" I have to shout so she can hear me as I watch her pull out keys to unlock an all-black Jeep Wrangler. If I could catch my breath I would scoff at how on-brand it seems for her.

"You wanted to come with, and this is how fast New Yorkers walk. You haven't learned that yet?" She's holding open my door just like Will, but this time I'm sitting in the passenger seat. I can't help but start smiling at the thought of sitting next to Eden again. This will be the closest we've been since Saturday's flight.

"No, but it seems like I could be learning from the best." The wink I throw to Eden just slips out as I get in and she closes my door.

I can't even look at her to see her reaction while she makes her way to the driver's side.

...

After a pretty uneventful and mostly quiet car ride, we finally make it to another warehouse building that just says "Bulk Foods" on it.

The whole ride I could barely get a "Mmhmm" or a "Yeah" out of Eden, and it's killing me to refrain from just yelling at her. I didn't expect her to actually ask me about the pastrami sliders because Kat was just being petty, of course. But, I definitely didn't expect to have to sit in silence.

As we approach two enormous garage-style doors, it's clear that this is the largest grocery store I've ever seen. Instead of regular grocery carts, everyone leaving is pushing massive flatbed carts, the kind you'd use for planks of wood.

"Where are we?" I ask. I'm so engulfed by the size of the store that I don't even realize Eden pulled out a membership card until I see an older woman wearing a purple vest scanning it. They're both staring at me as the woman flashes me a wide smile.

"First time here?" She asks enthusiastically. I quickly nod in response.

"Well, welcome to Bulk Eats! We've got everything your heart desires. But be careful darling, it's easy to get lost in here!"

I'm still staring at the endless aisles ahead as I turn around to say "Thank you," but Eden comes into view with one of the huge carts, and my eyes go wide.

"Do we *really* need one of those?" I question.

My naive question makes both Eden and the kind women throw their heads back in laughter while I stand there, in confusion.

When they both catch their breath, nobody answers me. She just smiles while still lightly chuckling, and Eden, already pushing the cart, walks past me.

...

I'm starting to get why my question was so funny when it's almost 8 a.m., and we're only halfway through the store, with our cart nearly overflowing. This place is insane. They have every ingredient you could dream of, in sizes that make you wonder who even uses that much. For a chef, it's like being a kid in a candy store—scratch that, a candy factory.

Eden has her own way of doing things. Every time she picks up something, it's like a well-thought-out move. She crosses it off her list and sticks to it. Whenever I grab something, I can feel her eyes on me. I've turned it into a bit of a game. It's not about the money—we both know she can afford anything here. It's more about control. She doesn't like me picking up random stuff just to look at it or toss in the cart without a reason. Everything has to serve a purpose, and right now, I'm having fun testing those limits.

I started off small, I purposely picked out all of the produce and ingredients that I was missing for my next recipe, before going completely off track. I picked up a bulk bag of Himalayan pink salt that I obviously didn't need, and just stood there for a few seconds before putting it back on the shelf.

Eden's energy immediately began to shift. I could tell she was annoyed that I was dragging this out by making miscellaneous stops in between, but I couldn't help but continue. So, I started to walk away from her knowing she'd have to follow me over to the candy aisle. But nothing was sold singularly so I'm currently looking at the twenty-pound bag of candy, and I knew Eden was going to have to say something.

With how the wheels screeched to a stop behind me I already started to smirk.

"Candy? Really?" She says with an annoyed sigh. I quickly fix my face before I turn around looking completely delusional to what's wrong.

"What? What's wrong with it?" My smile makes her eyes twitch and she looks like she's going to run me over with the cart.

"There's nothing wrong with it. Why the hell are we wasting time looking at things you're obviously not going to use?" Shit, this is the most I've gotten out of her all day. Who knew all I had to do was rile her up a bit?

"Who said I don't need candy?" I ask, barely holding back my laughter.

"Why in the world would you need *twenty pounds* of candy?" Her brows are raised. She's serious right now. I can't hold in my laugh any longer and I have to grab the cart to stabilize myself.

"You're too easy. Of course, I'm not getting twenty pounds of candy. Did you honestly think I wanted that?" I say, with my neck stuck out and my brows furrowed.

The silence and the slow nod of her head make my eyes widen.

"Shit, what kind of chefs were you interviewing before?" Finally, I get to see her chuckle a bit before we finally leave the candy aisle.

"You'd be surprised at what a chef will request you to have ready for them before they arrive."

Her lips are pulled tight giving me a look that means the list is probably endless. I can only imagine asking some of the most egotistical, self-centered people in the world "What can I get for you?" Just the thought alone makes my eyes roll for Eden. She and her team have had to deal with a lot I'm sure.

"Well, maybe you could tell me more over lunch, maybe?"

The cart comes to another screeching halt as Eden looks at me like I'm crazy.

"It's 11 a.m.?"

"Okaaaay, how about brunch?" I press. Her head shakes before she turns back around and starts walking again.

I continue, "Come ooon, I obviously don't have enough time to cook, get pictures done, and have your taste test today. And I'd say you owe me one for missing out on *two* interviews." I'm even shocked with myself when I finish, but I'm quickly reminded of my place when Eden's head tilts like she wants to reprimand me for raising my voice.

"Fine, but only after we finish shopping."

My eyes widen. It actually worked. Holy shit, I didn't expect her to give in. But I don't say anything else. For the rest of the shopping trip, I don't push or bother. I just walk behind Eden, letting her do her thing, because I got what I wanted.

CHAPTER 13

Riley

After scheduling the delivery of all the bulk foods, I'm practically seething with excitement as we make it back to the car. Eden, on the other hand, looks like she couldn't care less and would probably rather be *anywhere* else but here with me.

"What do you want to eat?" She asks passively. I turn to reply, but the movement of her right arm coming towards me stops me in my tracks. Her hand lands behind me on my headrest, and I let out a shaky breath as she backs out of the parking space.

Quickly thinking off the top of my head, I suggest with a smile, "Umm, well, you're the one that's probably reviewed every restaurant in New York to date, sooo take me to your favorite."

Her scoff comes out faster than expected. "I can't just take you to my favorite restaurant on a random Wednesday at noon." She doesn't even bother to cover up her rolling eyes. I don't either, because she's making this way more difficult than it needs to be.

"Why not?" I snap back.

Her head turns back to me, stopping the car in the middle of the parking lot. "You know, for a chef, you seem to not know much about this world. Or do all chefs in Vegas just not make reservations?"

Her eyes squint like they always do when she's trying to read me. I turn away with a nervous laugh—I'm not a chef, and it's becoming a bit too obvious for my liking. Quickly, I turn back to meet her gaze, trying to save face.

"Well, owning a restaurant in Vegas is completely different from here in New York. Besides, I figured the best reviewer in New York City would have some special in, to the best spots. Or has your rude approach burned all of your bridges?"

This time, it's her that's left speechless with an arched brow.

"I see you've done your research. And you still want to be featured in *Foodie*?" She says with a smirk after a moment.

She's back to driving, and I let out a small sigh of relief now that her eyes are off me. Every time she looks at me, it feels like I'm either going to burst into flames or confess every single lie I've told in the past week—both terrible options.

"Of course I did, I need to know what I'm dealing with, and after reading your work I like the challenge of impressing you. And you can't just scare me away." I protest. I probably shouldn't have admitted that I definitely stalked her before we met, because now she has this sick smirk on her face that does nothing but get under my skin.

When we pull up to the next stoplight, she finally turns to me, still smirking. "I can't?"

There's a moment of silence between us, and I can feel the air in the car getting thicker. "'Cause you seem pretty scared."

"Do you want me to be?" I ask, my voice low. Our eyes are locked in, and I feel closer to her than I did on the plane. I don't break our gaze, even as it feels like our seats are slowly inching closer together. But the blaring horn from behind us finally pulls us apart. Instead of responding, Eden presses the gas and continues driving.

...

After another thirty minutes, and thankfully not in silence since she turned on the radio to avoid continuing our conversation, we finally arrive at what I'm guessing is our destination. The entire building is painted black, which seems fitting for Eden.

"Where are we?" I ask. She completely ignores me, and I freeze when she reaches across me to push open my door. I don't even get a second to register what just happened when I see her hop out of the truck and head towards the entrance.

She wouldn't tell me anything besides the fact that we were going to go to West Village. As if that gave me *any* information. Now walking in, I barely catch a glimpse of the sign that says "Buvette", and now I'm even more confused than before. The space is packed with people, I can barely see anything besides the red brick walls, and what looks like a bar to the left.

Any other time, an atmosphere like this would make me anxious, but seeing Eden lead the way is oddly exciting. I'm caught off guard when she suddenly turns around and reaches behind herself to grab my hand. I try not to make any visible reaction, but she's already studying my face.

"Hey, you wanted me to take you to my favorite brunch spot in New York, at 11 a.m., with no reservation. Don't be scared now." She's smirking again.

It comes out like she's teasing me–testing me. Seeing if I'll back out. I straighten my back and fix my face.

"I'm not scared," I say calmly. Her smirk turns into a full smile, and it's captivating.

She turns back around without responding and pulls me deeper into the crowd. When I finally notice we've stopped, Eden is talking to someone behind the counter. The way their eyes light up at the sight of her tells me she's well-known around here. It's like Will and his connection to 'Katz'—everyone knows someone.

Within seconds, we're being guided through the restaurant to a much less crowded, open patio space. There are small red tables everywhere with chairs to match. The wooden flooring and green vines cascading down the brick walls make it feel straight out of a storybook.

But I'm not focused on the scenery anymore, because now I'm seated right across from Eden. I'm just now realizing we've never sat like this before. Both the plane ride and in the car we were side by side. Even when she tried my first recipe, she was sitting down and I was standing. Right now though, we're face to face for the first time.

Okay, it's more like face-to-chin, considering Eden is still taller than me even while we're seated. I'm instantly regretting my decision to go out to eat. And with Eden smiling and her legs crossed, clearly enjoying my fidgeting, it's obvious she's thoroughly entertained.

"Okay, here are your menus. I insist you try our 'Chef recommended' champagne, it pairs well with our Brunch, Lunch, and Dinner service."

For the first time, I actually noticed the tall blonde woman who Eden was talking to before she seated us. It looks like she's only talking to Eden, and I get why—she's practically foaming at the mouth. I don't mean to scoff at her eagerness, but Eden's head snaps towards me. Before she can try to read me any further, I clear my throat and turn to the waitress.

"Well, if you insist." It comes out a bit sarcastic and I have to look away to save myself from further embarrassment. I can hear Eden chuckle and say "Thank you" before the waitress rushes away. I don't waste time grabbing my menu to build a shield to cover my face. I can feel every muscle in my face relax for just a moment as I sigh. Fuck, this was a huge mistake.

"Are you jealous?" She taunts.

I quickly drop my menu and my cheeks are already turning red. "What?!" I try to whisper but it comes out a little louder than expected. Which just makes her laugh.

"I mean you practically made that waitress run away with her tail tucked between her legs. If you want more attention, use your words." She reaches for her glass of water to take a sip, while I sit there–gobsmacked.

"I'm sorry if the person who's supposed to be writing a huge article on *me* is giving more attention to the waitress than she has to me all week."

Okay, maybe I am just a little jealous, but rightfully so. The shift in her facial expression makes my tense shoulders drop and I fall back against my chair, not even realizing I was leaning on the table that separates us.

"Okay, I'm done with the teasing. I promise. And you're right, I haven't been as attentive as I probably should've been. I'm not normally like this, I've just had a lot on my mind recently–" She stares me straight in the eye when she says the last few words.

"–But that's no excuse, and I am so so sorry. I swear If you stick through this trip I can still get you an amazing article posted this weekend."

I've never seen her look at me this way before. Her eyes are soft, and she seems hopeful but apologetic. I immediately begin to shake my head at the thought of even leaving early, because it never crossed my mind. Even when she clearly didn't want to talk to me– I still wanted more.

"I mean, I guess I could stay and finish this article, but you've got a lot more to make up for." I'm teasing but Eden breaks out into a smile, and I can feel the energy between us already changing.

"Well, besides the fact that I purposely brought you to a fellow woman-owned restaurant, I think that should be a good start." My eyes go wide at the first thing she says, but my jaw drops when I follow the line of her hand pointing towards a waiter headed straight for us with a huge bottle of wine.

"Ladies, I have a bottle of Ponson Premier Pru. It's on the house, and I hope you enjoy it." I'm still in awe while he begins to pour our first glass, but Eden says "Thank you" before he walks away swiftly.

"Holy shit, did you actually scare that poor waitress away?"

We both look wide-eyed at each other for a moment before bursting into laughter. And for the next hour or two we let go of everything. We don't talk about the article, recipes, or anything serious at all. All we do is drink, talk about absolute nonsense, and laugh.

...

I don't know how many drinks I consumed, but by the time we were on the way home, my chef coat was halfway unbuttoned, and I couldn't stop the giggles that continued to pour out of me. Eden, of course, is completely coherent. She refused to drink any more than one glass because she didn't want someone else to have to pick up her Jeep.

And when we make it back to the Ritz, I'm nearly knocked out in the passenger seat.

I don't even know how Eden helps me up to my hotel room until she unlocks the door with one hand, making me slowly realize her other arm is wrapped around my waist, holding me up. But I'm so focused on her that I trip over the entryway rug and fall flat on my stomach, just like I did on Saturday.

I can barely get onto my hands before she hoists me up in one swift motion, causing my breath to catch in my lungs. We're face to face now as she guides me to my sofa, not even attempting to make it to my room.

As soon as I hit the cushions, my mind goes blank, and like most nights, my eyes are already shut. But before I drift away completely, I hear Eden mumbling under her breath, "You've got to stop getting in that position, you're killing me."

And I'm out.

CHAPTER 14

Eden

I knew taking her out was a bad idea, but I already felt pretty shitty about how I've been acting these past couple of days, and I needed to do *something*. I could've avoided all this if I had just come out of my office on Tuesday like Kat said. But no, I couldn't trust myself to be around her any longer than absolutely necessary. So when Kat called me out, I knew I deserved it. What I didn't expect, was for Spears to put me on the spot. I really didn't think she had the guts.

But when she looked at me, with a challenge in her eyes. Something changed. Like she wanted to see if I would play her game, it was beginning to feel like the tables were turning. And I had no other choice but to let her come shopping with me, or I would look like an even bigger dick than I already am.

At first, I had no reason to be worried. Besides her pit stops at random aisles—which I was starting to think she was doing on purpose to get under my skin—our shopping trip was going fine. But everything derailed when she said she was hungry because my subconscious instinctively knew where I wanted to take her the second she asked. In fact, I'd thought of bringing her here when I first found out she was Chef Spears.

I knew Buvette was the perfect choice because it is one of the only restaurants I still, to this day, speak highly of. Which says a lot, since most of my articles aren't the nicest, and not many chefs like me as a returning guest–understandably.

So, it was special to watch her relax, and talk like we did on the plane. Ever since then, I couldn't stop imagining what it would be like to take her out. To say this met all of my expectations would be an understatement. This was even better, being able to see her face-to-face feels like a dream.

From this distance, I can see her mood change in a matter of seconds–see the heat rise to her cheeks when I say something just a little more *out there*. Or, watch how quickly her head turns away when we look at each other for long enough. I never wanted it to end, maybe that's why I let the waiter bring over a bottle of champagne that I knew I wasn't going to drink.

Finding out she's not only a lightweight but also extremely happy when she's drunk makes wasting the day worth it. And as she continued to drink, I could feel my protective instincts start to kick in.

Even when I helped walk her up to her room, I knew there was no way I was going to let her go alone. And I sure as hell wasn't going to let someone else try to do it. The thought alone made me tighten my grip on her waist.

But I wish I'd held on tighter because when she fell like she did on the plane, my body froze. And just like before, she looked so good struggling to get up. I was tempted to stand there and just watch her.

This time, though, her eyes were slightly glazed over from the drinks, and the images of her played in my mind so vividly, like it had already happened.

I had to get out of there. After helping her up and onto her couch—because I couldn't bring myself to take her to her room—I bolted for the door.

When I finally made it home that night, I let the cold water from the shower beat against my hot skin, trying to wash away my feelings.

...

Thursday morning, I woke up feeling just as restless as before. If anything, my skin felt even hotter than it did last night. I hadn't gotten much sleep because every time I drifted off, visions of her would jolt me awake, leaving me in a pool of sweat. I couldn't bear the thought of taking a third shower before work.

And even after getting dressed, my suit didn't feel right. The fabric was itchy against my skin, making me feel like I was on fire. I would skip work and go to the doctor, but I don't think they have what I need right now.

And if I missed another day, Kat would serve my head on a platter and write an article about what a horrible person I am.

So, I pull my blazer off before entering the building, because nobody has time for my extra bullshit today. Plus, I already told Spears I was done hiding away in my office,–it's time to get shit done

Which is why I stopped by our local donut shop before work, so I could set them out on the conference table as a surprise. I refuse to fuck up another day.

...

Riley

Walking into the Test Kitchen, I'm blinded by the sun shining through the windows that wrap around the space. This is the first time the sun has been out my entire trip. Even through my headache, I take a moment to close my eyes and let the beams warm my face.

Today feels different. I can already tell. Maybe I'm just being overly optimistic, but yesterday was actually *fun*. Of course, I'm insanely embarrassed by how she had to help me back to my hotel room. If I could do that part over, I probably wouldn't have drank as much. I'll have to figure out sometime today to apologize for that, but I can't help but still feel like today is going to be a good day.

And when I finally open my eyes to see two big, famously pink boxes, I know I'm right. Half of the team is already busy working in the editing area, noticing they all have donuts on their desks already. So I pass by with a quick wave trying not to bother, but I hear Kat's voice coming from behind me.

"Hey! How was yesterday? Was Eden on her best behavior?" I can hear the concern in Kat's voice before I even turn around and it makes me chuckle.

"Hey! Yeah, it was great! I mean...it was chill, you know. I got everything I needed." I tighten my lips before I start to ramble, but a smirk is already forming on her face.

"That's it? It was *chill*? You guys were gone all day." Now her arms are crossed around her iPad, and I can tell she's not done questioning me.

"And Eden never buys donuts for everyone; you must have done something!" she says, eyeing me suspiciously. My eyes go wide as my head whips around to see Rach by the editors, trying to yell, "Yes!" in agreement with Kat. But she's also eating a chocolate donut with sprinkles, so everything comes out muffled.

All I can do is laugh and shake my head as I make my way to the kitchen, hoping this conversation will end.

"Oh, and by the way, your delivery came this morning. I already put the produce away for you!"

"Thank you so much, Kat! I really appreciate it!" She looks up from her 'To do' list to smile at me.

"It's really no problem, and whatever it is you're doing to make Eden this happy–please don't stop. You're making all of our lives easier."

I smile at her before she walks away already onto her next task. I highly doubt I'm making her life any easier, seeing as I'm not who I say I am. And her entire article is about someone she hasn't even met before. I can't think about that part too long without my chest starting to feel tight, and the room beginning to feel smaller. So, instead of diving deeper into my head–I find my zone and begin to get lost in the kitchen.

...

When I finally finish today's dish, I'm sweating. And not from running around, or even my explicit thoughts of Eden. My dish itself is physically opening my pores from the steam and burning my fingertips to the touch.

You wouldn't be able to tell by looking at it because, from an aerial view, the dense bed of fresh greens makes it appear as if there is nothing underneath. But in reality, this hot and spicy ramen is made with homemade rice noodles and an umami-packed broth, loaded with corn, tofu, and broccoli. Then, it's topped off with thinly sliced bok choy and kimchi before being completely covered in microgreens to resemble grass. Lastly, I use my tiny tongs that look like tweezers to finish off the dish, precisely placing edible orange and pink flowers where I see fit.

When I carefully bring my dish over to the photography studio, both Kat and Racheal are standing there with their jaws dropped.

"I'm calling it '*The Garden Of Eden*'."

I don't even realize what it is that I've said until I see both of their eyes look at each other before looking back at me, smirking.

"*The Garden of Eden*, huh? I wonder what made you come up with that one?" Kats' sarcasm makes me set the bowl of ramen down faster than when it was actually burning my hands. Luckily, nothing spills, but I'm already backing away from it like it's on fire.

"Yup! Now I gotta go– you don't need me here for this part, right?" I don't even wait for an answer before turning around to leave the room, but I'm quick to realize I have nowhere else to go. So I head to the first place I think of, and before I know it, I'm knocking on Eden's office door. My eyes widened knowing I've just dug myself deeper, thinking *this* is where I should go to escape.

But I can't turn away now, not when I hear Eden shouting "Come in!" almost like a command. The deepness in her voice makes my spine tingle and I immediately reach out to open the door and step inside.

Unlike the rest of the office, Eden's space was dim. The combination of her tinted windows and the curtains behind her desk pulled closed, make it almost pitch black. It takes a while for my eyes to adjust, but now I'm focused on the fact that Eden is sitting at her desk, her blazer completely off, revealing her tattoo-covered arms. And her skin is glistening, almost like she's been sweating just as much as I have.

"Hey, everything okay?" She asks. She must notice how frazzled I am.

"Oh, yeah! I was just coming to tell you, that I...ummm...just finished today's dish." Her brows are raised looking at my empty hands, which suddenly makes me feel so stupid.

"Well, they're still taking pictures of it, but I also thought I should apologize for how I was last night." My nervous laughter trails off into the silence before I try to turn to leave.

"Wait!"

I stop in my tracks.

"Could I get your opinion on this?" she asks, completely skipping over what I just said. I turn around and slowly make my way over to her desk, where she directs me to come around.

"So, I was going through the images Rachel took, and I wanted to see which of these was your favorite for the pastrami sliders."

I can feel my palms getting sweaty as I inch around her desk to stand right next to her–seated in her huge office chair. She moves over just slightly so I have enough room to step closer.

The images are incredible, but I can't focus on them right now. My body is nearly touching hers and I'm trying so hard to not look at her that I don't even realize she's finished talking.

"Sorry, what was that?" I mumble.

But when I finally turn, I can tell she's just as distracted. Her eyes are scanning over my face and they stop on my lips. I swear she can hear my heart pounding from outside of my chest. And before I register what's happening, I'm being pulled into her lap, and her lips are crashing into mine. The heat is almost overwhelming. I can hear the ringing in my ears. The kiss is rough, but passionate, like we've been waiting our whole lives for this moment. I can't stop, I feel like my body is moving out of control. My hips are jerking just from her hands on my waist, and I can't stop myself from ripping the clip out of her hair. We're a mess when we finally pull apart for one second to catch our breath.

"Fuck, I've been waiting to do this to you since the moment we met." Eden pulls my hair out of its low bun, and I moan in response.

Her hands move fast unbuttoning my chef coat, and I raise my arms to rip it off with my undershirt in one motion–revealing my black bra. It's almost like Eden is in a daze, I actually start to whine, already losing my patience.

"Please Eden, fuck."

Her eyes are back on mine and a mischievous smile stretches across her face.

"Take these off–now," she demands, motioning to my pants, coming out like an order, not a question. I've never moved quicker in my life.

"Fuck, you're lucky we don't have enough time, or I would bend you over and eat you out right here."

I practically jump back into her lap, but before I can do anything she grabs my wrists and pulls them behind me. I thought she was trying to push me off of her, but she tightens her grip and holds my wrists with one hand behind my back. And before I can question she's spitting onto her other free hand and reaches down to tease my already wet heat before slowly slipping two fingers inside.

"Oh fuck, Eden!" I can't stop the words from spilling out until she pulls out of me and I verbally groan in response.

"You need to be quiet, do you understand?" Her eyes look like they could cut through me, and all I can do is nod my head shakily.

"No, open your mouth and tell me you understand." The shift in her tone makes my eyes shut for a moment.

"Yes...yes, I understand." I sound breathy and needy, but fuck–I am. I drop my head back when she slips back inside of me, and I can feel myself relaxing as if she was meant to be here.

"Good, now ride."

My head snaps down to meet her eyes that are staring back at me, completely serious. She cocks an eyebrow, challenging me.

And that's all I need before I begin to use my knees to help me bounce on her two fingers that already fill me up. Once I get into a groove I let my body go, completely. My head is thrown back and I have to actually bite my lips to keep from screaming.

"Fuck, that's it. Come on my hand, I know you can." My eyes finally snap back open to see Eden watching me. She's always watching me, but right now it's different.

Her eyes look hungry, and not just for a snack. She's staring at me as if we were animals in the wild, she'd stalk me for miles in the dark and drag me home to feast on. Like I'm the prize, and there's nothing else like it. The thought makes my thighs shake, and I can't ride anymore.

But it doesn't matter, because Eden is already standing up, with my thighs wrapped around her waist–before immediately laying me back onto her desk.

Without removing herself from inside me, she begins to move fast and hard, slamming into the spot that makes my toes curl. My eyes shoot open in shock as she slaps her hand over my mouth before I can let out a sound.

I can feel her lips against my ear as she says "Just cum for me." And within seconds, my eyes roll back as I feel everything pour out of me.

CHAPTER 15

Riley

"So tell me, what was your inspiration behind this dish named *'The Garden of Eden'*?"

Eden's smile from across the conference table is almost hypnotizing. With how she's been teasing me, she knows I'm dying to crawl across this table to close the space between us. It's the only thing I've been able to think about since yesterday.

Even after Eden told me to go home early and rescheduled our interview for Friday morning, all I could think about was her. My skin felt like it craved her touch. I never even wanted to leave, but it was probably for the best before anyone got suspicious.

But now that I'm here, she's already pressed the voice recording app on her phone, and I can't seem to focus on her questions. Maybe because her hair is down for once, and every curl frames her face perfectly. And she's not wearing her blazer, *again*, which is making this much harder than it needs to be.

Her brows are raised, waiting for me to answer the question I've been avoiding ever since Kat first brought it up. I don't doubt that it's her eyes I feel burning into the side of my head from across the room, along with others wondering what I'll say. But I don't turn to look; I keep my focus on Eden's.

"Uhhh...well, the reason I made ramen in the first place is because I personally believe it's one of, if not the best, meals to have when you're in Vegas. There's nothing ramen can't cure. It's perfect if you're hungover from the night before, or if it's late and you're drunk and sad. A bowl of spicy ramen can seriously heal you."

Eden's smile grows bigger as I continue to speak. She doesn't interrupt or even move a muscle, she just observes.

"I named it that because of the presentation. Not only does it resemble a garden at first glance, but it represents the deception of something so beautiful, something you're not supposed to touch, but you just can't help yourself. And when you finally take a bite, it's not what you expected."

I realize I zoned out midway through and just said what I felt, which might've been a mistake given the way Eden is looking at me. Her brows are furrowed like she's trying to read deeper into what I said. Even though I know she doesn't truly understand, I can't shake the feeling that I've exposed myself, as if I revealed who I really am. Luckily, Kat rushes over and saves me from the awkward moment.

"Kind of sinister, but I like it! It's perfect for the article. I still refuse to believe that none of it is based on Miss Demon-Boss over here, but I'll let it slide for the sake of the review." My cheeks are already turning pink and I immediately look away.

"Kat! I'm in the middle of an interview right now!" I look over to see Eden glaring at Kat for interrupting.

"Uh, nooo, you're at the *end* of an interview. It's 12:30, You've been questioning her for hours now." And my head snaps to the right where the clock is above Eden's office.

Shit, I hadn't even checked the time since we sat down around 10 a.m. I figured it wouldn't take long, especially since it's technically my last day in the office and I've already cooked everything. But it's been almost three hours of me explaining what I can about Wendigo, without fucking up.

Now that it's over, I can't quite wrap my head around actually leaving. The days have flown by, and I've gotten so comfortable with my new routine. Foodie feels like what I've always wanted Wendigo to feel like. Will doesn't even seem like just my driver anymore—we talk like family.

My hotel suite is starting to feel like home. No, I still haven't slept in my room, but I haven't really thought much about it either.

I never really took the time to figure out what I would do when this was all done. I mean, I had an original plan–which was far different from what actually happened. But I got what I wanted, which was a good review of "Chef Spears."

So why do I feel so sad? I should be happy everything is finally done. I did it. I said I could do it, and I did. Every day I grew closer and closer to everyone here at *Foodie,* and it feels like my lies are just piling up. It's the little things, like when Eden says "Spears" instead of "Riley" that actually make my heart drop to the pit of my stomach.

Or, even when Eden took me to that women-owned brunch spot, just to try and make me happy. I wanted to scream right then and there, that I was just a horrible, crazy, prep cook that's been lying to her all week.

I've drowned in my thoughts when one of Kat's arms wraps around my shoulder. "I wish this wasn't your last day! You set the bar pretty high when it comes to the chefs we've worked with." All I can do is turn to offer her a small smile.

This is beyond bittersweet.

And when I finally look at Eden after some time, it feels like we may share the same feelings.

"Well, just know there's always a kitchen here in New York waiting for you." She gives my shoulder a final squeeze before heading out. I just now look around to see that everyone has left for the day. I guess we have been doing this for a while.

"Hey," I turn back to Eden, who's smiling at me, "do you wanna go somewhere?"

My brows furrow at her in confusion. "Where?" I ask. Now she's looking at me shocked but amused that I would even question her.

"Does it really matter? Besides, you never let me take you to my favorite restaurant for dinner." I can't stop the smile that spreads across my face.

"Wait, are you asking me out–on a date?" I ask with a grin as Eden throws her head back out of frustration.

"Are you just now realizing that?" She replies. I burst into laughter as Eden shakes her head.

"Is that a yes?" She prompts again. I stop laughing to look at her in disbelief. I can feel the hair on my neck start to rise from the anticipation–already beginning to grow. Holy shit. Eden Turner, the mysterious, stand-offish writer, wants to take me out on a *real* date.

"Of course," I say finally. And she's already smirking and standing up from her chair as if she already knew my answer.

"Good. I'll pick you up at six tonight."

...

After a painstakingly long drive back to the hotel I say goodbye to Will, and sprint through the lobby, all the way back up to my suite. I know I look absolutely insane and it's only nearly 1:00 p.m., but I haven't been on a date in...I don't know *how* long. And I only have five hours to look the best I ever have.

My suitcase is on the floor in seconds and I'm ripping through every single outfit that Izzie put together, just to find the only one I have in mind. When I finally feel the smooth, but structured fabric in my hands, I slow my movements, careful not to pull on it too hard. If I fuck up Izzie's pride and joy, then I might as well stay in New York–not that I would complain.

I rush to hang it up, and find the steamer to make sure it's absolutely perfect for tonight. Before I can think, I quickly grab my phone, snap a picture of the dress, and send it to my group chat with Joshua and Izzie.

Izzie is the first to respond.

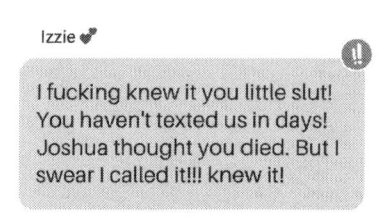

> **Izzie 💚**
>
> I fucking knew it you little slut! You haven't texted us in days! Joshua thought you died. But I swear I called it!!! knew it!

I can't help but gasp out loud. God, I've missed them so much. I know I've been MIA, but I really haven't had the time to check in. I've been so busy acting like Chef Spears, that I really never got a second to let my guard down completely.

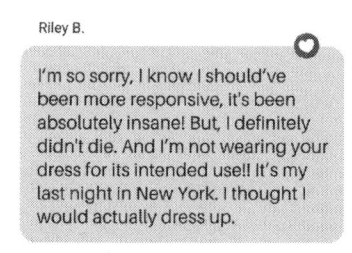

> **Riley B.**
>
> I'm so sorry, I know I should've been more responsive, it's been absolutely insane! But, I definitely didn't die. And I'm not wearing your dress for its intended use!! It's my last night in New York. I thought I would actually dress up.

I refuse to give her any information about Eden until I at least get home. Luckily Joshua finally responds, but he's no better than her.

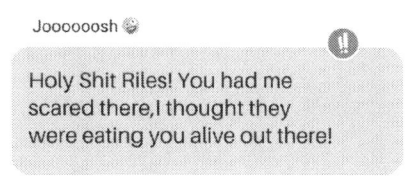

> **Joooooosh** 🐻
>
> Holy Shit Riles! You had me scared there, I thought they were eating you alive out there!

And now I can't stop laughing.

> **Izzie** 🌶️
>
> No! But someone was probably eating her out!!!

I immediately drop my phone and feel my cheeks begin to heat up–this is too much. *This* is exactly why I should have never sent that picture.

I hear a notification pop up on my phone and pick it up to see that Joshua has reacted to Izzie's text with a laughing emoji. I just roll my eyes. When another notification pops up, I don't waste any time—I immediately open the text and, without looking, start to type...

> **Riley B.**
>
> Please stop! Nobody's eating anyone out!!

I press *send* and toss my phone to the side. I can't deal with this right now, I need to get ready.

...

I planned everything out precisely. For the first hour, I spent my time in the shower mentally rejuvenating myself by washing away all of my thoughts from today. I've made it this far. What's the point of feeling like shit now?

Then, what should've taken me two hours, took three, doing my hair and makeup. I made the mistake of turning my TV to the music channel, and it went downhill from there.

But, I did try to keep it simple by doing a neutral makeup look with lip gloss. I finally ditched the low bun for curls, courtesy of Izzie's curling iron. I parted my hair straight down the middle and brushed the tight blonde curls out until they were more of a soft wave.

When I finally finished, I made my way out of the bathroom to check the time on my phone, to see a text from an unknown number.

Huh? I unlock my and click on the message. It

> **Unknown**
>
> Random. But, I mean, I wouldn't say nobody is.

takes me a few moments to realize what happened, but when I do, my eyes bulge out of my head.

My text.

My text that I thought I sent to Josh and Iz, in fact, sent to Eden *fucking* Turner.

She probably texted me hours ago, before I even started getting ready, and I must have opened it by mistake.

Oh my god.

My eyes scan over her texts so fast I can hardly read.

> **Unknown**
>
> Hey! I got your info from Kat. Hope that's okay! I have a gift for you waiting outside your suite, open it before I pick you up tonight.
>
> X
> Eden

I don't even know what I should focus on right now. The fact that I sent *the* most embarrassing text ever to Eden. Or, the fact that she was thinking of me enough to leave me a gift.

I choose the latter when I drop my phone and run over to the door, unable to contain my excitement. I almost tear the door off the hinges when I open it to see a small black box with a satin black bow on top.

It somehow seems just as mysterious as her. When I make my way back to the living room, I take my time unraveling the ribbon and removing the lid.

But, like many things with Eden, I'm left speechless and confused when I peek inside to find a small black silicone bean, nestled on a bed of black silk.

I pick it up to feel it in my hands, just from looking at it, I can tell it's around two inches long

But what is it? There are no buttons, no lights, and it looks exactly like a bean. I set it down and pick the box back up to try and find some instructions, but when I flip it upside down, a little note falls out. I'm quick to grab it, but when I finally read the thin cursive writing that I know is Eden's, my jaw drops to the floor.

Put it inside.

CHAPTER 16

Riley

"POISON"
By Brent Faiyaz

When I finally make it to the downstairs lobby, after wiggling into Izzie's surprisingly tight dress, I'm fifteen minutes late. Even with all the planning I did, I never considered the dress would have a built-in corset. So I had to figure it out by myself. I would say looking like a maniac pulling behind myself was worth it, though. I finished everything off with a champagne shimmer body oil.

The dress dips low in the front, revealing the most skin I've shown in years. The thin straps highlight my shoulders, while the dress clings to my body before falling away and flowing down to my ankles, stopping just above Izzie's thin strappy heels.

Walking through the Ritz, I'm so focused on counting my steps to avoid tripping that I almost walk right past Eden without noticing. I almost break my ankle spinning around to make sure I'm seeing correctly–it's Eden for sure. I wouldn't be able to mistake her curls for anyone else's.

She's wearing a suit, but she's never worn it like *this*. The blazer is completely open revealing an all-a completely black lace bustier. My eyes can't decide where to land. The matching slacks are high-waisted and flowy, the complete opposite of her usual, structured, straight-leg style. Though the pants are long, I can still see her sleek black heels peeking from the bottom.

I'm so overwhelmed I can hardly pull my eyes up to look at her face, which looks pretty amused as she watches me stumble around. Her eyebrows are raised as if she's waiting for me to snap out of my daze.

"Were you gonna just let me walk right past you?" I finally question.

A smile forms on her face as we get closer to each other. But she's not just looking at my confused eyes; she's scanning my entire body. I feel completely naked as if she can see every part of me.

"Yes, actually. It's a great view."

Her eyes finally meet mine and I can't think of what to say. I can see that same look of hunger growing in her eyes.

"But you're late." She continues.

My eyes narrow at hers, and she just raises a brow, signaling that arguing is pointless. She extends her hand, and after a brief pause, I take it. Without waiting for a second, she almost drags me outside. I'm still not used to New York's pace, and these heels make it even harder to keep up. When we finally reach the truck, she opens my door and places a hand on my waist as I step up into my seat. I feel that familiar tingle down my spine whenever she touches me.

She's in the driver's seat in the blink of an eye and the space between us is smaller again. I don't even need to go out anymore. The way we are sitting here in silence, just admiring each other, makes me want to turn around and take us back to my suite instead.

"You look absolutely breathtaking."

She's scanning my body as she says it, her hand moves to tuck a piece of my hair behind my ear, and the butterflies in my stomach are released.

"So do you." Our eyes meet and I see her smile widen.

"Did you get my gift?" She questions. This darkness sets into her eyes, and I can feel everything shift.

"I mean, yeah, but it wasn't really much of anything." My eyebrows are furrowed and I tilt my head waiting for more information on her inconspicuous gift.

But all she does is raise her eyebrows in response, "So you didn't do it?"

I sit in complete silence, turning to face forward in my seat to avoid looking at her. But I can feel her eyes on me, and I just know that sick smile of hers is growing. Luckily, she doesn't push any further and turns on the radio before starting the drive.

...

It wasn't long before we made it to our destination. We're in Time Square, at what looks like another hotel. I'm confused, but Eden's excited smile makes me follow her inside with anticipation.

I don't get a good look at the exterior because of how dark it is outside, but as soon as I step inside, I instantly recognize where I am.

I've never been here before, but I've dreamed of coming so often that it feels like I have.

From the architecture and design of the building, I can tell this is the "Queen of the Night" experience at the Paramount Hotel.

My mouth is gaping wide and the only thing I manage to say is "How?"

Eden's smile is bigger than ever and she looks satisfied with herself. "I wanted to take you to my favorite restaurant in New York, it just so happens to be a dinner and a show."

I don't even know what to say—I'm staring at her in awe. I've studied this place for years. I even wrote an essay about it back in school. It used to be a 1940s club. At the time I was writing my paper, the building was undergoing a multimillion-dollar renovation for the first time in over 60 years. The renovation aimed to create this interactive and immersive experience.

I've always been fascinated by the production and artistry behind such a massive project, but I never imagined I'd actually be here.

"Come on, we should get our seats." Eden grabs my hand and leads me down a flight of stairs where we are soon led by actors to our seats. From what I can see there are very few tables in the space, mainly because there is a huge stage in the center.

It's dim, but the small candle lit on the table between us adds a layer of intimacy. The purple and blue lighting gives everything a dreamlike quality, making it all seem too good to be true. When I look up and see Eden watching me, I can't help but blush. This moment is overwhelming, but I clear my throat and finally speak up.

"I'm surprised you brought me here, this doesn't seem like your vibe?"

She raises one brow and leans forward, "I like to have *fun*, sometimes."

I know she's not talking about the restaurant, but I don't get a chance to ask her more. The lights dim even further, and the chatter around us fades away. I look back at Eden, who's leaned back in her seat, smiling like she knows something I don't.

My gaze shifts to the stage as the lights turn red and music erupts from all around us. I focus on the performance, completely absorbed.

...

The show is incredible, nothing like I could have ever imagined. When the 'Queen' first appeared, it felt like a scene from a movie. Actors crawled across the floor like animals, creating an intense atmosphere. Some performed a strip tease on the larger tables, while others hung from the ceiling, nearly nude.

The energy in the restaurant was electric and sensual. The heat and sweat filled the air, and I found myself closing my eyes, feeling the rhythm of the drums pulse through my body.

Every time I would open them, Eden's always staring at me. The red glow that is cast across her face makes me fidget in my seat. And suddenly I'm reminded of her gift. I freeze in my seat. When I look up, she's grinning, like she was already thinking the same thing.

I straighten up and avoid her gaze by grabbing a piece of warm bread. I refuse to give in to whatever game she's playing. When I pick up my knife to grab some butter I stop in my tracks when I feel a sudden vibration. But it feels like it's coming from under me. Which is weird, because I thought I left my phone in Eden's truck.

I move to set the bread and knife down, but the knife nearly slips from my hands when I jerk forward. The sound of the knife clattering against my plate echoes through the room, but I barely notice. The vibrations have intensified, and I realize they're not coming from beneath me.

It's inside of me.

My eyes shoot up to meet Eden's, and all of the dots are suddenly connecting. She looks beyond amused. I almost choke up when I feel the vibration speed up again. I'm gripping the edge of my chair and my thighs are squeezed tight.

"Is something wrong?" Her smirk makes me glare. I can't even say anything because I'm too afraid that all that will come out is screams.

My eyes are pleading for her to stop, but it's almost like my body wants more. The people around us are too immersed in the show to notice me squirming around. I can feel it slowly move around inside of me, the vibration getting closer and closer to my favorite spot. My eyes start to flutter close.

But then the feeling is gone in an instant, and I have to stop myself from pouting when I open my eyes to see Eden with a raised brow.

"You close?" Her voice is low, just like when we were in her office. I start to move around in my seat and I almost give in but I like to have *fun* too.

"No," I lie, knowing I am on the edge of one of the best orgasms of my life.

I try to fix my face, but Eden can read me like the back of her hand.

"Oh, really?" Her confidence makes me roll my eyes. But when my foot kicks the leg of the table, I feel the vibration return, this time intensified. It takes everything in me not to throw my head back. My legs are crossed now, and Eden looks at me as if she knows I'm almost there. She leans forward, her face just barely illuminated by the candle on our table.

"Do it."

And like a switch, I let go. The vibrations stop, and I drop my head down as I feel myself come down. My muscles feel like jello and the only thing holding me together is this corset.

"Come on, we're leaving." My eyes snap up to find Eden already standing, looking at me the same way she did in her office.

She looks hungry.

...

We don't even try to keep our hands off each other when we make it back to my hotel. We practically raced each other down the hall before she slammed the door shut behind us. And suddenly this feels more real than before. There's no music, no lights–just us.

My suite is dark, and all I can see is her shadow against the front door. As it moves closer, I find myself backing away slowly. The sensation of being vulnerable and exposed, with her stalking me in the dark, makes my body go numb.

I can't even see her at this point, the shadow is gone, and my chest is starting to rise and fall much quicker. When I feel a soft hand grip the side of my back, I should gasp, jump, or even scream. Instead, I lean deeper into her. Her body heat envelops mine, and I feel her other hand wrap around my waist from behind.

"Are you scared?" Her voice comes out rough, but also soft. It's the perfect mixture, it makes my knees go weak and I have to make an effort to keep standing.

"No," I whisper. I hear her chuckle softly in my ear before grabbing my wrists like she did before.

"You should be." And with one hand, I feel her pull at the end of the ribbon to my corset loosening it almost completely. But before I can question she's using the same ribbon to bind my wrists together.

I'm in a state of shock when I feel her tie a bow and step away. As I try to move my hands, I realize not only are they stuck together, but they're also attached to my dress.

I'm about to turn around when I feel Eden's hands at my ankles, removing my heels. I step out of each one slowly, being careful not to fall forward. When she's done, she makes her way around and stands in front of me. Her curls look messier than before, and her blazer is off, giving me a full view of her breasts looking like they're barely contained in the black lace. I feel like I might be drooling.

She seems unaware of my daze when she finally speaks, "I just want to watch you."

"W-Watch me do what?"

Her hand moves to her pocket, and I watch as she pulls out something small and black.

I'm still trying to figure out what it is when she presses it, and the same vibration from earlier ripples through my body, making me feel like I'm about to fall.

"Stand up." She demands.

Her voice is firm and her eyes are hard. Even through the shake of my thighs, I plant my feet down firmly so I can get a better grip.

The vibration increases and I feel my eyes start to water as I break down.

"Please, Eden" I beg. She slowly walks toward me as she continues increasing the speed.

As soon as she steps in front of me, the rush fades, and I feel my body go limp. She wraps an arm around me, unties my wrists, and lifts me in one smooth motion, carrying me slowly toward my forbidden bedroom.

But for the first time, it feels right. When my body hits the bed it feels like I could float away on this cloud forever. My hands are on her waist as soon as she climbs on top of me.

The heat between her thighs feels like it's calling my name as she begins to straddle me. I can't stop my hands from grabbing a fist full of her curls before pulling her down onto my lips. Her moan is muffled as our tongues collide and I'm suddenly drowning in her.

The smell of her, the feeling of her–it's *everything* about her, that is driving me crazy. It's like no matter how hard I kiss her, it's never enough.

I finally pulled away for a moment to whisper, "I need to taste you."

Her eyes are wide as they scan over my face. But I have no room for embarrassment now.

"Please, Eden?" I beg.

I don't know how it happens but she flips us over in seconds, leaving me on top of her as she pulls her pants down. Of course, her underwear matches. I let out an audible groan just at the sight.

"Okay, but we're doing this my way–now flip around." My eyes are wide now, as she starts grabbing and flipping me around until I'm positioned with my knees next to her head and my face inches away from her heat.

"Sit down," she commands. I can't see her face, but I feel her breath against my heat as I slowly begin to inch back onto her tongue. I can't hold back the moan that rips through me as she pulls me back until her arms are locked around my thighs.

"Oh, fuck! Oh, fuck, Eden!" I cry out.

I have to physically break through her grip to bring my head back between her thighs. Pulling the lace to the side, I don't waste time tasting her. I've been in New York for almost a week, and I can proudly say this is the best meal I've had here.

...

We've been laying in silence for what feels like hours, just watching the lights sparkle from the window in my bedroom. I've never felt greater peace than laying here, in her arms. But that peace comes crashing down when I hear a ringing noise coming from the living room. I know it's her phone.

"Ughh! Just ignore it, please." I groan, gripping her waist tighter as I hear her giggle.

But the ringing doesn't stop; it continues to blare through the walls. As much as we'd like to ignore it, I finally give up and let her slip away.

"I'll be quick, I promise." She leaves a peck on my forehead before wrapping herself up in the sheet and scurrying down the hall. The ringing finally stops and I can hear someone else's panicked voice. I can only make out a few words but it sounds like Kat saying "I know it's late but…" And everything else is muffled.

The sound of Eden yelling, "WHAT!?" makes me jump out of bed and run down the hall, where I find Eden staring back at me in disbelief.

"What's going on?" I plead. My heart is racing trying to figure out what's happening. But my eyes flicker from Eden's face to the phone she's gripping so tightly.

"Who the fuck is Riley?!"

CHAPTER 17

Riley

"Flight 367 To Las Vegas, Nevada will begin boarding in five minutes. Please start lining up at your gate."

What do you mean, you're not Chef Spears?

"Ma'am?"

So you've been lying to me this whole time?

"Ma'am?"

Was this all just some game to you?

"Excuse me, Miss?" A hand grabs my shoulder making me jump. I look up to see an airport attendant looking down at me, she looks more concerned than anything.

"Oh, I'm sorry, what did you say?" I reply in a daze.

My head is whipping around confused, as I slowly come back to my senses. All of the passengers are already lined up at the gate, while I've been stuck, staring out the window, watching the planes preparing for take off.

"We're boarding the plane, Ma'am."

I don't know how long I've been sitting here imagining my body laid out on the runway. But counting planes has been my only distraction since I arrived almost four hours early. There was no point in staying at the hotel that I already didn't belong in. None of this was meant for me. I knew this from the start though, I knew how it could all crumble apart at any moment. But I was willing to risk it all for her.

Not that any of that mattered anymore. I screwed up everything. I lied to damn near everyone I know, *and* I fucked up the review. But worst of all, I hurt Eden.

I never wanted these worlds to collide, but I also knew it was inevitable. Granted, the ending could've had better timing. Apparently, while we were out, Joey sent an email to Kat apologizing again, for Chef Spears not being able to make it for the interview. She also wanted to check in and see how everything was going with me.

Something as small as an email changed everything in the blink of an eye. I felt so stupid. How could I ever think I could do this to these amazing people? The crack in Eden's voice as she screamed at me nearly tore me to pieces. But the cold emptiness I felt when she left before I could say anything was even more devastating.

And even though my flight wasn't until 5 a.m., when midnight approached, the only thing I could think of doing was going home. I knew that's what Eden wanted.

And I couldn't even imagine how low Kat thought of me now.

So after taking a shower, and awkwardly removing the toy from earlier, I packed everything up and called Will for the last time. Even that didn't feel right; someone so pure and genuine–driving a lying, fraud around. What a joke.

I wanted to leave at least one relationship from New York on a good note. So, when we said our final goodbyes, I kept my mouth shut about the lies and gave him one last hug. I might have held on longer than I deserved, but I needed it.

I thought boarding this flight would make me sad, but not flat-out distraught. Even as the still-concerned airport attendant directs me to my gate, everything plays like a record on repeat in my mind.

When I step onto the plane, my stomach twists at the thought of how all of this started. It's so similar yet so different all at the same time. I'm still in first class, with another window seat, but this time I don't feel giddy or filled with anticipation.

The seat to my left is empty, and all I can do is stare at it, visualizing Eden sitting there, working. I mentally add this to my ongoing list of things that are going to be the death of me. But the biggest problem currently topping that list is Chef Spears. I don't even know what to expect, considering Kat probably freaked out on him and Joey when she realized I wasn't who I said I was. And when I think back to the text Spears sent me right before I boarded the plane...

> Chef Spears
>
> Come into Wendigo as soon as you land.

I immediately order one of my complimentary glasses of champagne and sink back into my seat silently praying the plane will just swallow me whole.

CHAPTER 18

Eden

"YEAH YOU"
By King Sis

The sound of my apartment door buzzing wakes me up from some of the roughest sleep I've ever had. I don't even know when I actually closed my eyes, and I'm surprised I did at all.

But after last night's fiasco, I think my body just gave up. My throat is still dry from yelling at Spe–Riley.

After running around her suite like a maniac, just yelling and throwing my clothes on, I came home and cried for what felt like hours. I guess I eventually fell asleep.

But even then, I found myself waking up every hour, replaying each second of this week over and over again. Where could I have gone wrong? I feel so used and stupid. How could I have not known?

I mean who *does* that?

Fake your entire identity AND sleep with the writer, for what? An article? Or a new social status? Is that all I'm really worth?

All of these questions weigh on me, but I know they'll always be unanswered because–it's over. Whatever game 'Riley' was trying to play on me is over–she's gone. And in hindsight, she was here less than a week. How could I let this affect me this much?

Of course, I've had one-night stands before, but this was different. I've never mixed business with pleasure and now I see why you shouldn't. This all got so deep, so fast, and I didn't even know I needed to hit the brakes.

When Kat called me last night, I couldn't even respond—I thought it was some kind of sick joke. But when Riley couldn't look me in the eyes, I knew. Within minutes, I was gone. I couldn't bear to wait and see if she had anything to say. Why would I even hear her out when I don't even know who she really is?

Buzzzzzzz
Buzzzzzzz

The noise pulls me from my thoughts, and I groan, trying to cover my face with the blankets, but nothing drowns it out. Reluctantly, I climb out of bed and drag my feet across the cold cement floor.

When I decided to move into the apartment directly above the Test Kitchen, I thought it would make things more convenient. The layout is almost identical to the one downstairs. My home office is in the same spot as my office below, my bedroom is where the photography studio is, the dining and living room are in the area where the editors work, and the kitchen is an exact match to the one downstairs.

But as I walk past, I don't even spare it a glance, knowing all it will do is cause me more pain.

Buzzzzzzz

"I'm coming! Shit!" I shout.

My frustration is already reaching its limit, and I haven't even been awake for five minutes. When I pull open my loft-style door, I'm not surprised when Kat is standing on the other side. I definitely forgot to call her back after everything blew up. I should've known she'd show up banging on my door, especially after I finally took away her key.

"What the fuck, Eden? I've been calling you for hours!" She rushes by me and for the first time, I don't match her speed. All of my movements are slowed and every limb of my body feels heavier than usual.

"Sorry, I put my phone on silent when I got home." I finally meet her in my living room and flop down on the couch, while she stands in front of me, staring in silence.

"Okay, Eden. What do you want to do?" She finally asks.

"What do you mean?" I ask in return. The confusion has set in on my face as Kat looks at me with a raised brow.

"Well, you obviously can't sit here rotting in bed all day. The article is supposed to come out tomorrow. We don't really have time for this." She says impatiently.

I'm sitting up now, looking at her in complete disbelief.

"Kat, you can't actually be serious right now." She doesn't respond; she just tilts her head and places her hands on her hips.

"There is no article, Kat, it's over. Don't you get it? She's not even a fucking chef!" I practically scream.

Kat looks at me in disbelief.

"Is that really how you feel? You don't think she's a chef?" She asks without skipping a beat.

My brows furrow in confusion.

"What does that even matter? She lied to us, she lied to *all* of us. You should be *just* as pissed as me right now!"

I can feel my skin starting to heat up, everything is piling up on me and I feel like I'm going to blow.

"Don't get me wrong, Eden. She should've never lied, but be real right now–she cooked you some of the best dishes you've ever had."

My eyes drop to the floor, I know she's right.

"And after talking to the real Chef Spears, you should be happy you met the fake one. I'm just saying Eden, not everything is what it seems. Did you even ask her *why* she did it?"

That question makes my head snap up, and Kat is already looking at me knowingly. I hadn't considered how I didn't give her a chance to explain—I was too caught up in the chaos to think clearly. My flame is suddenly extinguished, and I can feel my shoulders drop in defeat. I don't even notice Kat sitting down next to me until her arm is around my shoulder.

"Personally, I've never seen you happier, and you know I will support you no matter what. But you need to decide, Eden: what do you want to do?"

CHAPTER 19

Riley

As expected, as soon as I arrived at Wendigo–I was fired. I didn't even try to act shocked. There was no point in arguing with him. It was bad enough I had to come in on a Saturday, right on time for brunch.

As I made my way through the packed restaurant towards his office, I didn't even try to find Izzie or Joshua. Now isn't really the time for a reunion.

When I first walked in, he didn't even look me in the eyes before beginning to tell me how he wasn't surprised this is how it turned out.

He expected it to all blow up somehow. For someone who just lost this chance at a huge article, he seemed pretty happy with the fact that I failed. He practically smiled with self-satisfaction, as if my failure was a bigger prize than being named "Best New Chef." I wanted to laugh in his face and tell him what a joke he was.

But in fact, I was the real joke.

Because he was right, I deserved every blow he threw. And even after he was finished and I walked out silently, it still didn't feel like enough. I still felt like shit.

By the time I got home later that day, it felt like everything was sitting in my throat. Every time I swallowed or took a breath, it felt like I was being choked. I know I looked fucking pitiful, rolling my suitcase into my apartment building with tears streaming down my face.

But it's time I really let it out. I'm finally home, and none of this fully hit me until now. After I lock the door behind me, I immediately drop to my knees. I can't stop the tears from flowing, and I don't think I really want to. I've been faking it for far too long already.

And it's all over. I have to start completely from scratch. Wendigo has been all I've known since school. What am I going to do now?

I don't know when I'll actually get the chance to cook again. Spears will probably drag my name through the mud, and word travels fast in Vegas. I doubt any restaurant will even want me to wash their dishes after this.

When I finally manage to peel myself off the cold hardwood floor, I can only muster enough strength to crawl onto the couch in the living room. I curl up into an armadillo position, wishing this nightmare had never happened.

After a few hours, I know it's Izzie walking in because the lock is so old she always has to wiggle the key three times before it actually opens. I instantly regret choosing the couch to decompress, but I don't have the energy to open my eyes. I flip onto my side so my back is facing the front door. Even though I haven't seen her in days, I'm still not ready for any more human interaction.

She seems to get the hint because, within minutes, I feel a blanket draped over me. Her hand briefly rubs my arm before I hear her heading down the hall to her bedroom. I seriously don't deserve her or Joshua.

All they've done is try to support me through everything, even if it meant faking my identity. They've both been there for me.

Eventually, I fall asleep, with my mind playing clips of Eden working on the plane. It seems to be the only thing that calms me enough to stop tossing and turning.

...

I'm jolted awake by the blanket being ripped off me, the cold air hitting my body so suddenly that my eyes snap open to find Izzie and Joshua standing over me.

"What the fuck?" I spit out. My eyes are still adjusting to both of them, but they don't seem to care.

"Okay, Riles. We get that the whole situation with Chef Spears was crazy, but we're not going to let it consume you." Izzie's voice is so bright it almost feels jarring compared to how I'm feeling. But I still don't understand what's going on.

"Yeah, come on. You really can't be stuck on that dickhead when you have so many new opportunities now." Josh seems to match Izzie's optimistic energy, and I couldn't be more confused.

"I mean–if you could have seen his face today! Riley, when I say that, he was pissed!" He adds.

Before they even finish speaking, they burst into laughter. I'm still at a loss as they both seem to be rambling.

I sit up and attempt to take control of the situation.

"Hold on. What time is it?"

I rub my eyes before looking up to see Josh staring back at me with his brows furrowed and his eyes wide. I'm just now realizing that they're both in their work uniforms.

"Bitch, it's almost 6 p.m. We just got off work."

My eyes practically bulge out of my head. "Shit! It's Sunday?"

Izzie exaggerates, nodding her head as if she's trying to say *'duh'*.

I didn't realize I'd been asleep all day. I never even heard Izzie leave for work this morning. I guess all of this really has taken a toll on me.

"Are you just now waking up?" Joshua's eyes look like they could pop out at any second.

"I mean, yeah, I'm not really in the bes–"

"Wait, so you haven't seen the article yet?" Izzie looks like she wants to strangle me.

My face twists in confusion. "The article?"

Now they couldn't look more annoyed with me, but Izzie doesn't respond. She runs down the hall and returns with her laptop already open and typing. I'm even more lost than before.

When she turns the screen toward me, the bright white light is almost blinding. I squint as I read the title, and my eyes widen with every word...

A STAR ON THE RISE: CHEF RILEY BENNETT'S CULINARY BRILLIANCE

CHAPTER 20

A STAR ON THE RISE: CHEF RILEY BENNETT'S CULINARY BRILLIANCE

By Eden Turner, Editor-in-Chief of Foodie

*I*n the city that never sleeps, Las Vegas, Nevada, where creativity and luxury often collide: a new star has emerged from an unexpected place. Originally, this article was meant to be a piece written on Chef Spears, owner of the new and fresh fine-dining establishment called Wendigo. But because of an unusual mix-up, I was lucky enough to meet Chef Bennett, who, at just 24 years old, has worked as a prep cook and fruit sculptor at Wendigo for 2 years.

Although I wish we'd met under different circumstances, everything happens for a reason. I was given the privilege to try all of her amazing creations that demand recognition.

Wendigo, known for their lavish brunch, and high-profile guests is not exactly the kind of place where I expected to find this hidden gem. But that's exactly where Bennett's journey began. Underappreciated, yet unyielding in her craft.

If you've read any of my past work, then It's obvious I've never been much of a fan of Las Vegas restaurants. But during her time in our test kitchen, Bennett demonstrated that her artistry extends far beyond the fruit carvings she would meticulously make. For example, when she first presented me with a dish I'd like to call Deconstructed Candy, I thought she was insane. But she was actually a genius. The crack of the candied shell, combined with the bright flavors of the fresh fruit, creates an experience all on its own. Her dishes are a testament to her creativity, precision, and innate understanding of flavor. This dish not only reflects her roots from working at Wendigo but also showcases her unique creativity.

But Bennett's talents go far beyond the canvas she's given. Her exploration of flavors and presentation are highlighted within my favorite dish—The Garden Of Eden—a hot and spicy ramen with tofu, broccoli, and corn. It was served with kimchi and bok choy before being topped off with an enchanting bed of microgreens and edible flowers.

The result was a harmonious blend of spicy, savory, and earthy notes that transported me out of this world. It was a dish that could easily find itself on the menu of any Michelin-starred restaurant, and yet it was crafted by a young chef, still early in her career.

When asked about her inspiration for the dish, Bennett states, "I named it The Garden of Eden because of the presentation. Not only does it resemble a garden at first glance, but it also represents the deception of something so beautiful—something you're not supposed to touch but can't help yourself. And when you take a bite, it's not what you expected."

Unfortunately, I never got the opportunity to try her mouthwatering, mini pastrami sliders. My team's hands were much quicker than mine. Bennett's version of a classic comfort meal featured thinly sliced, and lightly charred pastrami. And from what I heard, her bread was the star of the show. The handmade sweet rolls paired beautifully with the smokey and hearty pastrami.

But besides her work, what is perhaps most remarkable about Chef Bennett is her resilience and adaptability. Unbeknownst to me, she transitioned from the role of a fruit sculptor, where her work was often overlooked, to becoming, in my eyes, a rising star in the culinary world. This shift speaks to her determination, vision, and passion.

At an age when many chefs are still finding their footing, Riley Bennett has already made a name for herself, and her journey is just beginning. If her time in our test kitchen is any indication, the world can expect great things from her in the years to come. She is a force to be reckoned with, and I, for one, am excited to watch her rise to even greater heights.

EPILOGUE

"HOME"
By Ballah

8 months later

"Hey Chef, where do you want these?"

The smell of thyme and garlic melting with European butter puts me in a trance and everything around me seems to become muffled.

"Chef?"

My head snaps up to see a crate full of strawberries being pushed into my face.

"Oh, uhh...can you take it to the back, please? And, can you see if Ivan has started on the chocolate fondue for dessert?" I look up to see Blair, our prep cook, nodding her head in understanding.

"On it." She replies, and she's gone within seconds.

I turn back to my pan, being careful not to let my garlic burn. This butter will work beautifully with tomorrow's breakfast. But I'm quickly distracted when I see a figure leaning against the wall next to me.

I almost jump out of my shoes. "Shit, babe, you scared me! What are you doing back here?" My eyebrows furrow in confusion as I whip my head around, only to see two cooks working on the last course for the night.

I just sent out the last round of hors d'oeuvres: bacon-wrapped four-cheese jalapeño poppers. They were the perfect follow-up to my honey-sriracha glazed chicken, which was paired with lemon-garlic roasted asparagus and a bright mango salsa. From the sounds coming from the front, it's clear that everything was a hit.

I turn back to Eden, but she's closer now and lowers her voice, saying, "Do I really have to stay in the front if I'm the one fucking the chef?" My eyes widen as she smirks at me.

"Well, I guess there could be exceptions," I reply. Her smirk grows into a smile and I can see her eyes begin to darken. I'll never get over that look, it sends chills down my spine–every time.

"Yeah?–" I watch as her eyes scan the semi-empty kitchen. "–How much time do you have before the last course?"

My eyes bulge as I scan her face, unable to tell if she's serious. She doesn't look like she's joking; her eyes are locked on my lips. I don't even realize I'm turned towards her completely until I smell something burning. My head snaps back to the stove, and of course, the garlic has turned into garlic chips, and I've completely browned the butter.

"Shit!" I quickly move the pan off the stove, hearing Eden laugh behind me. I glance over my shoulder to glare and roll my eyes at her.

"Well, there goes my garlic butter for tomorrow." Her laughter only gets louder.

"Sorry, babe, didn't know I could distract you so easily." I can hear the smirk in her voice, she's clearly not *that* sorry.

"I should get back to my table anyway, I wouldn't wanna miss dessert." When I finally turn back around, Eden wraps her arms around me, and I immediately melt into her embrace. It doesn't even take a minute for me to forget about her making me burn the butter. All I can focus on now is the feeling of her arms pressing against my back and her lips enveloping mine. I can't help but let out a low moan as our tongues collide.

"Hey, you whores! I know this is your restaurant and all, but can you save it 'til Opening Night is over with?"

I break away from Eden and turn to see Izzie with her hands up in the air and her eyebrows raised, I can't help but laugh. It's been a blessing having her work as the front-of-house Manager.

After the *Foodie* article blew up and I announced I was opening my own restaurant here in New York, almost everyone at *Wendigo* quit. It just wasn't a good look, being known for working for Chef Spears anymore. I haven't spoken to him since he fired me, but after Joshua finally moved out here he told me Spear's has completely lost it.

"And aren't *you* supposed to be in your seat? I mean, come on people, this is a civilized establishment!" Izzie's voice reminds me of a sergeant and Eden raises both of her hands in the air as if she's been caught.

"I'm out, I'm out, I promise." Eden throws a wink at me before Izzie follows her back out to her seat.

And I can't help but stare in awe, because I finally feel–home.

Keep reading for a special preview of the next romantic comedy by Taylor Riley Parham.

AT YOUR DOOR

CHAPTER 1

MIA

"Umm, excuse me?"

I can hear a high-pitched voice coming from behind me but my hands are drenched from washing out one of the blenders, and I'm not really in the position to talk to customers right now. But I can already hear the layered conversations coming from all directions, which can only tell me one thing–it's 6 a.m.

In San Francisco, at that time, all anyone cares about is coffee. Doesn't matter your background, your industry, or how much money's in your bank account—coffee runs the city.

And for the next few hours, we'll all swap roles, jumping in to help put out each fire as soon as it sparks. So, even though I'm supposed to be cleaning, I drop the blender in the sink, slap on my Disney smile, and turn to face a blonde woman juggling a stroller in one hand and a small Vanilla Frappé in the other.

"Hi, can I help you?"

Her light scoff as she looks me up and down doesn't go unnoticed, "Uh...yeah, I ordered a Vanilla Frappé with no whip, but this clearly has whipped cream. And my baby can't have all that sugar."

I can feel my teeth grinding as I hold back from telling her there's more sugar in that Vanilla Frappé than in a can of soda. Not to mention the caffeine they pretend isn't in it, even though it's been on the menu for years. Yet, moms like her come in here every day, proudly buying it for their kids.

"Let me fix that for you?" I reach out to grab the drink and she pulls away at the last second.

"Can you actually remake the whole thing, please?" It's not really a question. I nod, forcing a semi-tight smile, and there it is—that same sick look only specific customers give me. The kind that screams, "I'm above you." It used to crush me, but now I'm practically immune.

So, I turn away and remake her sugar-loaded, caffeine-packed Vanilla Frappé, no whipped cream, still smiling. When I turn back, she looks anything but happy, seeing me handle it without a problem.

Here ya go! Sorry about that." I can feel the wave of self-satisfaction already coming over me.

"Mhmm, thanks." And she's gone within seconds.

I only get to relish in my small success for a moment, before I hear an all too familiar yelp come from across the room, and I quickly turn around to find Eleanor flat on the ground covered in milk.

"Cold foam?" I ask, knowingly.

Her eyes are closed but all she does is nod her head. I don't know how many times I've found her like this, but it's slowly becoming a habit. I bite back a giggle before reaching my hand out to pull back up and we both stand there watching as the puddle of milk spreads across the floor.

"Don't you *dare* laugh!"

"I'm not, I swear, I'm not." But I know my face says otherwise.

"Come on and help me before Joe notices, he can't know I fucked up my 5th batch."

Her whispering reminds me that the shop is still packed with customers waiting in line, and panic starts to set in as I look around and realize there are only a few of us on the floor.

"Okay, go grab a new apron while I clean this up. We need to get started on those orders." My eyes are zeroed in on the amount of empty cups—with names written on them— lined up on the counter.

El's head whips around to see what's caught my eye, "Oh, fuck meee!"

I've been working at *A Brew For You* for almost four years now, and I still can't get over how fast things go from totally fine to a complete shit show. But as I watch El dash to the back while I clean up this spill, I realize I wouldn't want to do this with anyone else.

We've been best friends our whole lives, and when it comes to making coffee, we're the best duo. Maybe that's why Joe's kept us around so long—or he probably just figured he could pay two broke introverts next to nothing while still having us work full-time.

And it's worked, for quite some time, clearly. Of course, there have been times when we both said "Fuck it, let's quit!" But in reality, it's the best option for me right now.

For one, my 300-square-foot apartment is in the building that sits right on top of *A Brew For You*, making it the shortest commute of all time.

And secondly, I couldn't imagine having to start completely over at a new job. Just the thought of having to sit through an interview makes me sick.

When we were first hired, desperate for anything, our social anxieties were thrown out the window. Behind the counter is probably the only place I don't feel like I'm going to die when someone talks to me. Or like every word that comes out of my mouth is going to just crumble up into dust. I feel calm, and unlike others, I like the early mornings. The cold and crisp air combined with the smell of fresh coffee beans is magic in itself.

El would much prefer to sleep in, but we both know we work better together. We keep each other on track, force each other to show up, and then when we're done, we rehash all of our embarrassing moments from the day—usually over takeout, upstairs in my apartment.

Which is what I'm trying to convince El to do when it's finally time to clock out at noon. But I can already tell by the frown on her face, that she's going to say no.

"Why not? Let's watch a movie!" I whine. I try to make the sad puppy dog eyes at her as we walk out the front door towards her baby blue Subaru.

"Ugh, I wish, but my family's in town for my nephew's birthday, and you know how my mom gets. She needs my help preparing the food and probably anything else she can think of." Her hands are waving around in the air as she unlocks her car.

"Yikes. Well, tell Noah I said 'Happy Birthday!' And text me when you make it home." I pat the hood of her car before stepping back onto the curb.

"You too!" El says jokingly. We're both laughing as we go our separate ways.

When I finally step into the small entryway of the old building, my body starts to relax as I slip into cruise control, ready to begin my end-of-the-day routine. I turn to the right and use my key to check the mailbox. Aside from a couple of coupons, it's completely empty.

Locking it again, I glance up at the narrow spiral staircase and let out a deep sigh. The elevator's been broken since I moved in, but every day, I still glance to the left at the metal gate covering it, hoping that maybe, one day, it'll be working again.

But for now, I turn back towards the old, creaky, wooden stairs and begin my journey all the way up to the sixth floor. Which up until recently, occupied only 4 residents.

Probably because the elevator is broken, and you'd have to be either crazy or desperate to want to make the journey up here. I know I'm both, and my neighbor Mary who lives across the hall isn't crazy, she just really wanted a view of the water. And my neighbor Alex—who travels the world half the time backpacking—lives an insane lifestyle so I count him as crazy. But the one person I have yet to figure out is my new next-door neighbor.

I've been lucky enough to avoid her so far, but judging from the loud music and constant voices coming from her apartment these last few days, I doubt we'd get along.

She's clearly a loud, party girl who doesn't care about anyone else, and I'm the complete opposite—I like peace and quiet.

Maybe it's because I don't really have friends besides Eleanor, and sometimes I play *Uno* with Mary, but she's partially deaf in one ear and I'm still learning sign language, so our conversations are limited. Either way, I enjoy my alone time, and lately, that's been ruined. Today's no different. As I round the corner and step onto the sixth floor, I can already hear the music spilling down the hallway.

"Great." Is all I can mutter out as I bend over with my apron and bag in hand, barely keeping it off the ground, as I try and catch my breath.

When I finally muster the strength to keep moving, my eyes lock onto the apartment straight down the hall. Past mine, past Mary's, past everyone's. It's the biggest apartment on this floor—a two-bedroom I've had my eye on since I moved in years ago.

Unfortunately, like many of the apartments in this building, it's been vacant due to construction and plumbing issues. I don't know the specifics, but if it's anything like the maintenance needed in my own place, I doubt it'll ever be available. Not that I could afford it anyway, but that doesn't stop me from dreaming.

I'm completely knocked out of my daze when I feel my body lurch forward after my foot gets caught on something. I'm barely able to catch myself with my hands before I crash into my front door.

When I finally regain my balance, I immediately look down to find the culprit. I'm even more confused to find a medium-sized brown box sitting in front of my door.

"Huh?" I'm standing there with my eyebrows furrowed as I try to think over my past few purchases. My eyes suddenly go wide, wait, is that what I think it is?!

I ordered it just a few weeks ago, so it really shouldn't be here yet, but I know it's the only thing I've ordered in a while.

When I finally pick it up, I'm sure it's the one. The box isn't too heavy, but it's definitely not filled with feathers. I can hardly contain my excitement as I unlock the door, kick it closed behind me, and hurry to my coffee table to set everything down. Fortunately, I keep a box cutter nearby. As soon as I see apartment number 444 on the shipping label, I don't hesitate before tearing open the seal.

I ordered it months ago on Etsy after seeing Eleanor eyeing them in a store, and I immediately started saving up to get it for her birthday coming up. I was worried it wouldn't arrive in time, but as my hands rip open the flaps of the box and toss aside the tissue paper, I can't contain my smile when I finally pull out a...

DILDO?!?!

ABOUT THE AUTHOR

Taylor is a matcha-loving, romance-writing Virgo, enjoying every moment in the vibrant city of Las Vegas. When she's not crafting spicy queer love stories, you'll find her curled up with a good horror movie or usually with her nose in a book.

Though a proud homebody, she loves exploring her city's art scene. Taylor's days are a blend of creative inspiration, cozy comforts, and spontaneous city adventures. At home, she's kept company by her sweet 4-pound Chihuahua and two playful cats. Stay connected and follow her journey at @authortriley.

Made in the USA
Columbia, SC
01 May 2025